Heat jolted through her at the sight of him—big, strong and intense.

His dark hair was slicked back in a stubby ponytail that made him look subtly dangerous, and he'd shed his heavy jacket to reveal the broad shoulders and muscled arms beneath his dark green sweater.

He slapped a file folder on the table and said, "Okay. Let's get this over with."

His voice had a rough growl that fired Jenn's blood even further, reminding her of how he'd sounded right after they made love. But even as her heart thudded at the memory, Nick glanced up at the one-way glass...and looked nothing like the man who'd made love to her.

No, the man on the other side of the glass was cold and hard, with a faintly derisive edge to his tight-lipped smile.

A sinking shiver took root in her belly.

That was definitely Nick in there—it was his body, his face, his presence—but it wasn't the man she knew. This Nick had an aggressive jut to his jaw and moved with an unfamiliar swagger. His eyes held none of the alert intelligence she was used to. Instead, he was cold and chill, with a demeanor that practically screamed, "Go ahead and impress me. It won't be easy."

JESSICA ANDERSEN

BEAR CLAW LAWMAN

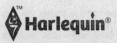

TORONTO NEW YORK LONDON
AMSTERDAM PARIS SYDNEY HAMBURG
STOCKHOLM ATHENS TOKYO MILAN MADRID
PRAGUE WARSAW BUDAPEST AUCKLAND

Recycling programs
for this product may
not exist in your area.

ISBN-13: 978-0-373-69630-7

BEAR CLAW LAWMAN

ABOUT THE AUTHOR

Jessica Andersen has worked as a geneticist, scientific editor, animal trainer and landscaper...but she's happiest when she's combining all of her many interests into writing romantic adventures that always have a twist of the unusual to them. Born and raised in the Boston area (Go, Sox!), Jessica can usually be found somewhere in New England, hard at work on her next happily-ever-after. For more on Jessica and her books, please check out www.JessicaAndersen.com and www.JessicaAndersenIntrigues.com.

Books by Jessica Andersen

*Bear Claw Creek Crime Lab

CAST OF CHARACTERS

Jennifer Prynne—A newcomer to Bear Claw's crime lab, Jenn is determined to prove herself in the face of a questionable past. She never intends to fall for a sexy undercover agent…or become the target of a criminal mastermind who has developed a taste for murder.

Nicholas Lang—The DEA hotshot should be focused on closing the case and getting back to his work, but he's distracted by Jenn's independence and curvy good looks. Their affair blazes hot and heavy before it crashes and burns. When she becomes a crucial witness in the case, though, who better to protect her?

The Investor—The criminal mastermind's militia has been broken, his drug operation crushed. So why is he still in Bear Claw…and why is he hunting and killing his former underlings?

Slider—The Investor's lackey has a lead foot and few scruples.

Tucker McDermott—The head of Bear Claw's homicide division knows Nick too well to believe the dedicated DEA agent will turn his back on his Miami home to stay in the Wild West.

Gigi Lynd—The crime scene analyst is Jenn's closest friend in Bear Claw, but she's a huge romantic at heart and refuses to believe that Jenn and Nick aren't meant for each other.

Matthew Blackthorn—The acting mayor is facing a crime wave and huge budget issues, but he has faith that the Bear Claw P.D. and its crime lab are going to be the key to saving the city. Hopefully.

Chapter One

Normally, Jennifer Prynne would've been glued to the task force's bimonthly meeting, taking notes on the latest developments in the Death Stare case and trying to think of new avenues the crime lab could explore. Today, though, she couldn't make herself focus, not just because there weren't any major developments, but because she had something far more interesting to think about.

Or, rather, some*one* far more interesting.

While Chief Mendoza went over stats that said the police crackdown was working, with fewer and fewer Death Stare ODs trickling into the local hospitals, Jenn glanced a few rows over to where Nick Lang sat with a couple of homicide detectives, comparing notes in an undertone.

Nick's home base might be in sunny Florida, but the on-loan DEA agent blended seamlessly with the cops of Bear Claw, Colorado. Even though he'd only been in the city for twelve days now, he was wearing layers against the early winter chill and had a heavily insulated bomber draped over the back of his chair. His quick, intense blue eyes were all cop, and as he leaned in to say something, the others got quiet and listened.

But at the same time that he blended, he stood out, too. The men around him didn't have his jaw-length, raven-black hair or economical way of moving, and their bodies didn't give off the same sense of leashed strength and deadly control.

Not to mention that the sight of them didn't made Jenn's pulse kick up a notch, in a way it hadn't done in a long, long time.

A nudge in her ribs startled her, followed by a blush when Gigi—her friend and fellow crime scene analyst—whispered, "You're staring."

A few months ago when Jenn had first come to Bear Claw, recruited to her dream job by her old friend Matt Blackthorn—who was Gigi's fiancé—Jenn might've stammered an apology or tried to pretend she was paying attention to the briefing. Now, though, riding high on hormones and happiness, she just raised an eyebrow. "D'ya blame me?"

Gigi's glance went to the side of the podium where Matt was sitting. He was acting as the city's interim mayor after the former mayor and his deputy had been indicted as conspirators in the Ghost Militia. But Jenn had a feeling that Gigi was seeing only the man when her eyes softened and her lips curved, and she said, "Nope. I don't blame you one bit, because when it's right, it's damn near perfect."

Jenn couldn't help smiling in return, but she shook her head. "It's not like that."

She and Nick had been clear on that from the beginning—he was only in town for a couple of weeks, so there was no point in starting something serious. And besides, neither of them was looking for anything long-term. They were just having fun.

Lots and lots of fun.

Gigi rolled her eyes. "I've seen you two together. Trust me, it's exactly 'like that.'"

Not letting herself acknowledge the inner glow that brought, Jenn focused on the front of the room, where Mendoza had yielded the podium to Tucker McDermott.

Tucker was head of the Homicide Division and leader of the task force that had finally broken the Ghost Militia's hold on the local drug trade. After a few brief words of introduction, he started listing the top dogs who were still at large—including the mastermind, a shadowy figure known only as the Investor—and bullet pointing the search for the fugitives and any remaining drug-distilling operations that might be out there.

Although the park service had shut down access to the diseased trees that formed the basis for the Death Stare compound, the word on the street was that there was still a mother lode of the highly addictive—and extremely deadly—drug out there somewhere.

"In other, better news," Tucker said with a grin. "Last night we got the go-ahead from the DEA to keep Nick Lang with us here in Bear Claw for the duration of the case."

What?

As Jenn sucked in a breath, Tucker kept talking, saying things about the valuable perspective Nick brought to the team and how he would be continuing his street-level efforts to ferret out the last of the militiamen and, ultimately, the Investor himself. But she barely heard any of it over the sudden buzz of blood in her ears.

"See?" Gigi elbowed her again. "When it's right, it's right. He must've leaned on his bosses to let him stay so the two of you can have more time together."

"Or, hello, because he wants to help bring down the Investor." But Jenn couldn't squelch her silly-stupid grin, so she ducked her head to hide it. She and Nick weren't keeping their fling a secret, but there was no reason to go around broadcasting that she was doing inner handsprings right now.

"Either way, looks like he's going to be sticking around past this weekend."

"That's what the evidence suggests," Jenn quipped. And whether or not she wanted to admit that she'd been counting the days he had left, she couldn't be happier. She snuck a look over at Nick, and found him accepting a couple of back slaps, and nodding and grinning at something the officer behind him had said.

Her whole-body glow notched up at the confirmation. It was real. He was staying.

Gigi followed her eyes. "He didn't mention it to you?"

"Nope." Jenn made herself look away as Tucker started talking about the trail that Nick had been following through the shady contacts he'd already cultivated in the short time he'd been in the city.

That was what he did best. He made friends, gained confidences and got the gossip. That was part of what made him one of the DEA's best undercover agents. That, and his ability to make the worst-of-the-worst criminals believe he was one of them.

Strangely, the rumors rife on the streets and in the back alleys of Bear Claw said the Investor was still in the area even though he'd lost his manpower, his political pull and most of his equipment. Nobody could figure out why he would've stuck around, but the police force was following up on the rumors, hoping to hell that something would pan out and they would finally be able to nail the smart, slick criminal who had nearly destroyed Bear Claw over the past year.

Most of the leads would turn out to be dead ends, of course—the local criminals who had made up the Investor's mercenary army had become convenient boogeymen, and were being blamed for everything from petty theft to murder. But for every twenty dead ends there might be one nugget of truth. And sometimes that was all it took to crack a case.

Jenn loved that part. And over the past couple of years, when she'd been away from crime scene analysis, she had missed it more than she'd wanted to admit. She might not have the world's strongest stomach when it came to the actual crime scenes, but she rocked in the lab. She loved the rush she got when the pieces came together and helped put criminals behind bars.

As Tucker finished up and swapped places with another senior detective, Gigi leaned in and whispered, "Nick probably wanted to surprise you."

"He succeeded." Jenn wouldn't have pegged him as the kind of guy to go for such a public surprise…but then again, she didn't really know him all that well.

Not yet, she thought with an inner smile, then glanced over when Nick rose, grabbed his bomber and headed for the far door. He had his cell in his hand and was reading a text message as he walked—no doubt something from one of his contacts—but he paused at the door and looked back, meeting Jenn's eyes.

Heat skimmed through her, but she played it cool and just cocked an eyebrow. *Well?*

He tapped his phone, then slung his coat over one

shoulder and pushed through the door, easing it quietly closed behind him.

A moment later, her cell vibrated and a text appeared: Gotta make some calls. Meet me in Interrogation 3 when the meeting's over.

Gigi read it over her shoulder and made quiet *hubba-hubba* noises.

Jenn shushed her. "You're going to get us in trouble."

It was an empty threat, of course. With the kind of multitasking required in the crime lab, it was a no-brainer for the two of them to listen to the reports while teasing each other. Besides, every single member of the task force knew the value of a little friendship and stress relief at times like this, when they were working a high-profile case that was plagued with far more questions than answers.

Not to mention that Jenn had already earned a good, solid reputation around the lab, even though she was still in a six-month probationary period. Although Matt had personally vouched for her, the higher-ups in the Bear Claw P.D. hadn't exactly been enthusiastic about hiring someone with her background. Still, she had the necessary experience, the city was broke and she was willing to work for a fraction of her worth in order to get out of the paternity-testing snooze zone and back into a crime lab, doing the work she loved.

Even better, she loved it in Bear Claw—loved the people, loved the city—and she was determined to earn a permanent place in the Bear Claw crime lab. But that didn't mean she couldn't have a little fun on the side, as long as it didn't interfere.

"Catch up with me later," Gigi said as the meeting wound down and the task force members started to disperse. "I'd like to have you take a look at a couple of soil samples."

Jenn nodded. "Will do."

Although all of the analysts in the six-person crime lab could handle a scene, they each had their strong suits when it came to the nitty-gritty: Alyssa was a whiz at facial reconstruction; Maya was a profiler; Cassie knew all the latest and greatest advances in DNA; Ravi was the local bugs-and-beasts expert; and Gigi was their crossover to active duty, with SWAT training in addition to a pedigreed résumé in crime scene analysis. Jenn was hell on wheels, literally: tire tracks, footprints, soil samples and other assorted smudges were foreign languages for her to decode—sometimes it took a while, but she could usually figure out what was going on, making her invaluable in the lab.

"And besides," Gigi shot over her shoulder, "I want to hear how the 'interrogation' goes!"

Jenn laughed and waved her off. "I'll see you later."

Stowing her cell in the pocket of the trim brown leather jacket she'd left on against the chilly air—which was only going to get worse as the winter wore on—Jenn grabbed the rest of her gear and headed for the far hallway, which led to the interrogation rooms.

As she slipped through the same door Nick had used, giddy flutters took root in her stomach and she was suddenly very aware of the weight of her jacket and the way the sleek lining of her wool trousers slid across her skin. And when she reached Room Three, she paused for a second with her hand on the knob. *Take it easy,* she told herself. *Play it cool.*

Not that this was a game, of course—they had both been up-front and honest with each other from the very beginning about what they wanted and what they could give. But that was before a first date that had them up and talking until sunrise, a third date that had culminated with the best sex of her life and a fourth date that had seen them moving his things out of the hotel and into her apartment because there didn't appear to be any point in wasting the department's money for the remainder of Nick's two-week stint in Bear Claw. Which, it seemed, had just been given a stay of execution.

Letting out a long, slow breath and trying not to be too obvious with the happy-happy-joy butterflies, she pushed through the door into Interrogation Three.

The fifteen-by-twenty, gray-painted space, with its table and chairs, mirrored window and surveillance camera, should have been stark and unrelenting. But with Nick standing with his back to her, watching their reflections in the one-way glass, it became intimate instead. She saw his eyes in the mirror, saw him track her as she crossed the room and tossed her things on the table next to his bomber.

She moved to stand beside him, liking the pair they made in the mirrored glass. She was a good eight inches shorter than his solid six feet, and had wavy brunette hair and curves that contrasted with his big, lethal body. Even their eyes were different—hers alight with interest and anticipation, his level, almost reserved. Cop's eyes.

Nerves stirred, but it was just his work face, she knew. Trying to meet him halfway on that one, she bumped him with her shoulder, coworker to coworker. "Hey. Way to give a girl the heads-up that you're going to be sticking around. Guess I should lay in some more buffalo burgers."

Two weeks ago, she'd had nearly ten pounds of the

stuff in her freezer, leftovers from a late-fall barbecue. Now she was down to three lonely patties, thanks to her and Nick's habit of planning to go out for food, but then getting otherwise occupied in the bedroom. Or the couch. Or wherever. She'd been watching the supply dwindle as the days counted down, figuring they'd both hit zero at the same time. Now, though, she thought it would be nicely symbolic—whether he knew it or not—to replenish the stash.

Except he wasn't grinning at the inside joke. He was staring at her in the mirror with something more than reserve in his expression now. Something that looked an awful lot like guilt.

The butterflies took a dive. "Nick?"

He cleared his throat and turned to face her, so those killer eyes were looking down at her, guarded and, yes, guilty as he said, "Listen, Jenn…we need to talk."

And all she could think was, *Oh, hell.*

WE NEED TO TALK. For years now Nick had thought those were the worst words a man could hear, not because of what they meant, but because of what they symbolized—problems, issues, changes….

This was the first time, though, that he realized as much as it had sucked him to hear the words, it ripped him up even worse to say them to someone else. Especially someone like Jenn.

She'd come into the room ready to celebrate, but now the light dimmed in her chocolate-brown eyes and the color drained from her face, making the sprinkling of freckles on her cheeks and nose stand out. "You didn't ask your bosses to let you stay longer, did you?"

"No, I didn't. The DEA wants the Investor in custody before he hits any other cities with the Death Stare."

"What about you?" she asked. "What do you want?" And damned if her voice didn't crack a little on the last word.

"I…" He trailed off, guilt stinging at the sudden sign of vulnerability.

She wasn't supposed to be vulnerable, darn it. She was supposed to be gritty, tough and self-reliant—he wouldn't have gone after her in the first place if she hadn't been. More, she had been totally on board with the no-strings short-term fling that was all he ever offered. Heck, she was the one who'd brought up the ground rules in the first place.

They'd wound up getting in way deeper than that, though, and from the look in her eyes, the lines had started to blur for her, far more than he'd suspected.

Nick cursed himself inwardly. He should've stuck to his no-overnights policy, should've put the brakes on when things first started to slide. He didn't like that he'd let things go as far as they had, didn't like how his normal control had slipped. And he hated doing this to her now…but there was no way he could let things keep going the way they had been, or worse, let them go further.

"I want…" Damn, this was harder than he'd thought it would be, and he'd known it would be hard—that was why he'd kept putting it off, not telling her there was a chance he'd be staying until it was an absolute done deal. He was paying for that now, though. "Tucker found me a two-room apartment around the corner that I can rent by the week. I'm moving in there today."

"You're breaking up with me." Her voice was a monotone, her face a pale mask.

When he'd gone over it a hundred times in his head, he'd planned on saying something about how they'd agreed it was just for a couple of weeks, reminding her that they had promised when it was over, that they would walk away with no hard feelings. But they had already gone too far beyond where that would've made sense, so he just nodded. "I'm sorry, Jenn. I wish—"

"Don't." She held up a hand, snapping that hard-eyed, determined mask of a poker face back in place. "Just don't, okay? It's… It's like we said—a couple of weeks of fun. It's been a couple of weeks, and tomorrow would've been goodbye, right?"

He nodded, though he wasn't sure it had really been a question. "Right."

"Then there's nothing more to say." She turned away to snag her stuff off the table, then stood there for a moment, shoulders stiff. He couldn't see her face, didn't know if she was fighting tears or anger, or both. Her voice was steady, though, when she said, "Don't worry about any rumors, or seeing me around the station. I can handle it."

He winced, but couldn't think of anything he could say that would make things better, and figured he shouldn't try. The situation was the situation, and they were both going to have to get through it as best they could until the sting wore off or he went home, whichever came first. "I'll come by after work and get my things."

She nodded, still with her back to him. "Okay. I'll see you later, then." She hesitated, but when he didn't say anything else, she headed for the door without another word.

He told himself to stay put. Instead, he caught the door on its backswing and stood at the threshold of the interrogation room, watching her walk away.

Her strides were loose and limber and her shoulders were square beneath her butter-soft leather jacket, and she walked—as she always did—like she was ready to take on the world. That was one of the things he'd first noticed about her, the way she was always up for any challenge, any experience. He'd liked that about her. Hell, he'd liked damn near everything about her.

"You did it, huh?" Tucker said from farther down the hall.

Nick exhaled as Jenn took the stairs heading down to the basement, where the crime lab was located, and disappeared from view. Then he glanced over at the big, rangy detective. "Yeah. I did it."

He hadn't meant to bring Tucker into things, but they had been friends a long time. Tucker had been the one who'd recruited him into the case, and he'd been the one who dropped the "congrats, you're staying in Bear Claw until we catch the Investor" bombshell the other day…so he was the one who'd gotten the whole story—or most of it, anyway.

Tucker glanced back in the direction Jenn had gone. "You want me to give Alyssa the heads-up, ask her to make sure she's okay?"

Nick told himself to leave it alone. Instead, he nodded. "Yeah. But don't tell her why I did it."

Tucker sent him a sidelong look. "You sure?"

"Leave it alone." Nick inhaled, trying to fill the empty spaces. "She's better off without me."

"What about you? Are you going to be better off?"

"That's not a priority. I'm just here to help close the case."

Tucker didn't look convinced, but he shrugged and held out a sticky note. "Then you're going to want this."

Nick took the paper and skimmed the address written on it. "What's the deal?"

"That's what I need you to figure out. Looks like we found one of the lieutenants…or what's left of him."

Chapter Two

One month later...

"This one looks even worse than the first two," Jenn commented from the doorway, breathing through her mouth and doing her best to see the scene in terms of the evidence it might provide, rather than what it said about the victim's last hours of life.

The ME's office had collected Chuckie Dennison's corpse, but what was left behind was plenty gruesome in its own right. Everything from the dining room chair—which had ropes sagging off it and a series of fingernail scrapes where the victim had struggled to free himself—to the array of kitchen utensils and small hand tools meticulously spread out on the stained burgundy tablecloth, said that the victim had been brutally tortured.

Gigi, who had gotten there first and started methodically photographing the scene, let the camera hang at her side as she took a look around and grimaced. "We'll need the autopsy to be sure. But, yeah, it's bad. And, yeah, I think you're right that it fits the pattern. Odds are that it's the Investor again."

That was the word on the street, anyway. The rumors

said it was the mastermind himself who had hunted down two—now three—of his former lieutenants in the Ghost Militia. The men had been found tortured to death, with the scenes showing every sign of an ordered, organized and ruthlessly self-controlled killer. Nobody knew whether the Investor was disposing of potential witnesses, getting revenge, or what.... Or if they knew, they weren't telling.

Which meant that the task force was dealing with three bodies, three crime scenes and lots of evidence, but they still didn't have a name or description of the Investor, and no idea when or where he would strike next. The former members of the Ghost Militia weren't the type to ask for police protection; in fact, the last few remaining higher-ups had gone even deeper underground after the killings started.

"You don't think it's a vigilante?" Jenn asked as she set down her field kit, gloved up and got to work on the chair, which Gigi had already photographed.

That was the other theory the cops were working on, that it wasn't the Investor at all, but instead, a local who was hunting and killing the remaining members of the Ghost Militia. Unfortunately, the list of people with possible motives was all too long—eighty-three people had died from Death Stare overdoses, and another dozen innocent bystanders had been killed during the Militia's last desperate struggle to escape from the crackdown. Although many of the dead drug users had been among the city's homeless, meaning that some had been tagged with just a first name, or sometimes not even that much, others had been ID'd. Which meant there were hundreds of bereaved family members out there, even more grieving friends…some of whom might be inclined to take matters into their own hands.

But Gigi shook her head. "It's a plausible theory, sure, but I'm going with the word on the street. Nick… um, the task force's connections have a pretty good track record so far."

Jenn's cheeks heated, but she made herself concentrate on the ropes that had been used to bind the victim, photographing them from even more angles before cutting them free and bagging them. After a moment, she said, "You can say his name, you know. It's not like I don't see him around."

The dubious look Gigi shot her spoke volumes about just how bad Jenn had been at camouflaging her disbelief and unhappiness for those first couple of weeks after Nick dumped her. Or, at least, how bad she'd been at hiding it from Gigi and her other friends down in the crime lab. As far as anyone else knew—she hoped—it hadn't been at all obvious that she had been hurting.

She was damn good at making it look as if everything was okay, after all. And in the fine tradition of "fake it until you make it," eventually the sting really had worn off.

"I'm fine, really. I'm over it." Jenn sealed a bag and signed her name on the first line of the label, starting the evidence chain. "It wasn't even about him, really… it was everything." She filed the bag in her kit, then rocked back on her bootie-covered heels to look over at her friend.

She hadn't really talked about the breakup, even with Gigi, partly because she'd needed to work it out for herself, and partly because she'd hoped it would quickly become old news.

It didn't seem to be, though—Gigi and the other analysts still looked at her with pity in their eyes every time Nick's name came up or, worse, when they crossed paths. Which wasn't that often, granted, but when they did, she knew that the others were watching her, waiting to see how she would react, as if she hadn't been a hundred percent professional the last dozen times it had happened.

Not that she was counting.

"Everything?" Gigi nudged. Finished with the photographs, she was using a laser device to measure the room and the big pieces of furniture.

Those details, along with the photos and other notes, would go into one of the computers back in the lab to make a rendering. It wasn't quite the kind of high tech used by the crime scene shows on TV—those were largely a combination of science fiction and reality, anyway—but it was more than most local police departments could boast.

Unfortunately, even the money Matt was funneling into the crime lab couldn't force the case to break.

Jenn hesitated, then shook her head and got back to work, donning fresh gloves and getting ready to start swabbing the gruesome stains on the chair. Odds were that it all belonged to the victim, but it was still worth doing the work. That was the name of the game with crime scene analysis: ninety-nine percent drudgery and one percent *eureka*.

She worked methodically, swabbing each spot, retracting the swab into its sterile sheath and stoppering and labeling the tube, so if—or rather, when—the Investor made it into court, there wouldn't be any chance of the evidence getting thrown out.

Not this time, she thought grimly, all too aware that over the past month, the case had gotten very personal for her, both as a way to prove herself, and a way to make amends for some of her past mistakes. Including the one she'd made with Nick, letting herself get distracted from what was really important by something that they had both agreed from the very beginning would only be a passing thing.

It wasn't anybody's fault but her own that she'd let herself forget that part.

Aware that Gigi was waiting for an answer, Jenn finally said, "Nick wasn't the first guy I've dated since Terry died…but he was the first one who made an impact. He was the first one I was excited to see, the first one I missed when we were apart, the first one—" She broke off. "Anyway, even though it's been almost three years since Terry was killed, Nick was my rebound. I jumped in too far too fast, and clung too hard to something that wasn't real, mostly because I was so damn excited to finally feel *something*."

"The thing between you and Nick was just a rebound, huh?" Gigi's tone didn't quite call her a liar. But it was close. "And now you're over him. You sure about that?"

"One hundred percent." Not just because she needed to be, but because she was seeing him for who he really was these days. Over the past month, without the blinders of lust and admiration dimming her view, she had realized that the man she had known—the one she had thought she knew so intimately—was just one part of the real Nick Lang…and she wasn't sure she liked the other parts of him.

With her, he had been charming and courteous, but with an edge of wicked and earthy humor that had jibed with her own, along with a down-to-earth streak she'd loved. He'd made goofy faces at Amber, the K9 who'd taken up desk duty at the P.D., along with her injured human partner, Kelsey Meyers. He'd gone running in the rain with Jenn and he'd used her shampoo without caring that it made him smell like flowers. And when she'd gotten up in the middle of the night to pace or stare out into the darkness, when she came back to bed, he'd always stirred and reached for her in his sleep.

She might not have known where he grew up or what kind of music he liked, but she had thought she knew what kind of man he was. That is, until she started watching him more objectively and realized that while he was sometimes the guy she'd gotten to know, he could also be any number of other guys, depending on the situation.

With the other cops, he was a cop, which made sense. But she had also watched a couple of tapes of him interrogating some of the jailed militiamen. And what she'd seen had startled the heck out of her, because he hadn't just been talking with them, he'd *become* one of them—not just with a few quick changes of clothing, but with his body language, his speech…. Even his face had been different, though she couldn't have said how. More, she'd seen him do the same thing on other tapes, with witnesses. He'd been the perfect gentleman with a nervous grandmother and a midrange escort, but toughened up fast when facing a trio of teens who'd thought they were more badass than him and very quickly learned they were wrong.

She'd watched the tapes in order to get a different context for her evidence, in the hopes of adding to the case. Instead, she had learned more than she'd really wanted to about Nick.

He was a chameleon, the kind of guy who could slip into any situation and make himself indispensable. He'd even said as much, though not in so many words, when he'd told her that his greatest skill as an undercover agent was his ability to slip into any group, any situation. But what worked for busting drug rings really didn't work for her.

That wasn't resentment talking, either, or an effort to make herself feel better about the breakup. If anything, it had made her feel worse to realize that she'd come very close to once again falling for a manipulator.

Her instincts, it seemed, still sucked.

"Anyway," she said, realizing the conversation had lagged, though she'd kept swabbing at the bloodstains, capping and labeling the tubes with automatic precision, "I'm grateful for what happened, in a way. At least I know that part of me isn't gone for good. Getting involved with Nick showed me that I can feel those feelings again. I'll just have to make sure I use better judgment and next time around find myself someone who's really available and not just passing through."

"Does that mean you'll let me set you up?"

Jenn winced. "Look, I'm sure the bird man is a great guy—"

"He's an ornithologist, not to mention Matt's best friend. He's really cute in an intense yet geeky sort of way, and I think you guys could have some fun together…." Gigi trailed off hopefully.

"I…well, not right now, okay?"

"When?"

Seeing that Gigi wasn't going to give it up—she was

still in that slightly sickening, more than slightly annoying "everyone should be as happy as me" phase of her relationship—Jenn blew out a breath. "After the Death Stare case is closed. Until then, I want to stay focused on this." Her gesture took in the scene and the spatter, and for a moment the smell intruded, bringing a stab of pity for a man who probably didn't deserve it, followed by a sting of guilt that she was letting Nick distract her again, and he wasn't even in the room. Or her life.

Gigi sent her a long look. "You know what I think? I think that—" Her phone chimed, interrupting with the two-note tone that said it was incoming info from Dispatch. Jenn let out a sigh of relief as Gigi answered with, "Go for Gigi." She listened for a moment, then nodded. "I'm on my way."

"Please tell me it's not another torture victim." The Investor—or whoever was doing this—had never hit twice in one night before…but he'd also never shed this much blood before, or used his makeshift weapons with such vicious abandon.

"No, but it's related." At Jenn's look, Gigi grimaced. "It's a murder-suicide, guy and his girlfriend. Looks like he was flying high on Death Stare, and snapped before he OD'd."

"Oh." Jenn swallowed an uncharacteristic surge of nausea. "Damn it. I thought it was off the streets."

"Apparently not all the way." Gigi took a look around, lips flattening. "I hate to leave you here alone." The analysts tried to work in pairs, but it wasn't always possible.

Jenn waved her off. "I won't be alone. There are plenty of cops in the building doing door-to-doors."

"That's not what I meant."

"I know." Gigi was the only one who knew how

much the actual on-scene work bothered Jenn. But it was a part of the job, and one she'd learned to tolerate. "Go on. I've got this. We've nearly finished the first sweep, anyway. Another hour, maybe less, and I can take this stuff back to the lab and get started on the preliminary runs." That was the part she was good at, and where she could make a difference for the case... and the victims.

Gigi was already packing her gear, of course. They didn't really get a say in where they went, or when. "You don't mind taking all of it back with you, mine as well as yours?"

"Not a problem. If I need to, I'll get one of the cops to help me carry it downstairs."

"Promise me you won't try to do it all yourself?" Gigi's tone was suddenly intense.

Jenn looked up at her friend. "What?"

Wearing her heavy parka now, cheeks flushing from the heat in the apartment, Gigi shrugged and looked a little sorry that she'd said anything. "I just...I don't know. It worries me that you keep so much to yourself. I want you to know you can talk to me...or if not me, then Matt. Or someone."

Not sure how they had gotten here, Jenn rocked back on her bootied heels. "I'm fine, really."

"You keep saying that."

"Because it's true." Or close enough. And the parts of her that weren't fine weren't the sort of thing her new friends in her new home could help with. History was history, baggage was baggage, and she needed to deal with it herself. "Thanks, though. I mean it."

Gigi wavered for a moment, then exhaled. "I need to get going. Damn that drug."

Relieved by the change in subject—though equally frustrated by the situation in Bear Claw—Jenn said, "We're going to get the bastard, Gigi. One of these days he's going to make a mistake and we're going to get him."

Granted, that wouldn't fix things for the victims who'd already died, or their families. But still.

Gigi headed for the door that opened from the small apartment into the fifth-floor hallway. She stripped off her booties and gloves in the doorway and took a long look back at the scene. "I hope to hell we get him soon."

"Me, too." Jenn lifted a hand. "Keep your eyes sharp." It was a saying from her old crime lab, one of the few things she'd brought with her to Bear Claw.

"You, too. And don't forget to have someone help you carry that stuff down." With that, Gigi let the door swing shut behind her and her booted footsteps moved off down the hall.

Jenn blew out a long, slow breath that didn't do much to ease the tightness in her chest as she found herself alone in a dead man's apartment.

On one level it was a relief to have Gigi—and her probing questions—headed somewhere else. On another, though, her departure sucked the life out of the room, letting the smell crowd closer, until the atmosphere felt thick and cloying, like it was sticking to Jenn's skin.

"Get a grip," she muttered. "You wanted to be back working in a crime lab, and you got what you wanted. Now deal with it and do your job."

It took her nearly an hour to process the main sitting area, where Dennison's murder had taken place. With the knives, tools and tablecloth all documented, labeled and packed away, she moved into the victim's bedroom.

This particular crime scene was unusual in that the victim was also on the P.D.'s most wanted list, which meant she wasn't just looking for evidence that would help them identify his killer, but also anything that might lead them to the other fugitive militiamen…or their leader.

It was a complicated case, both challenging and frustrating.

The cops had already searched the other rooms, but she was seeking less obvious clues. And although the *aha* moment of an analyst finding exactly the right strand of hair sitting alone on an otherwise pristine carpet was pure Hollywood fiction—the reality was more along the lines of dust bunnies and dead ends—there were occasional *aha* moments in real life, too.

Her instincts quivered over some papers wadded in a wastebasket next to the bed, and again over a pair of boots lying near the closet as if they'd just been kicked off. They had dirt embedded in the treads…and that was her kind of evidence. Figuring out where the victim had been prior to his death could be very, very useful, and that was just the sort of thing she could do using the soil.

Maybe. Hopefully.

Whistling softly under her breath, she headed out into the main room and crouched down to rummage at the bottom of her kit for a larger evidence bag. The creak of the hallway door behind her shot adrenaline into her system and had her heart bumping, but logically she knew who it had to be.

"Gigi told you to come up here, didn't she?" Straightening, she turned toward the door. "Well, I'm not ready—"

A man rushed her and slammed a fist into her face.

Pain exploded alongside shock and Jenn reeled back with a scream. Her foot snagged on her evidence kit and she fell. Her heart hammered as she grabbed the kit, tried to roll away, tried to get away, crying, "No! Help! Somebody *help me!*"

He followed her, wrenched the evidence case from her fingers and then grabbed her by the hair with brutal force. She caught a glimpse of lethal gray eyes and a thin-lipped mouth before he slammed her head into the floor. And the lights went out.

Chapter Three

Nick paused on the landing and stuck his head through the stairwell door for a quick survey of the fourth floor, one level below the victim's apartment. A couple of doors down, a uniformed officer paused midknock, then relaxed. "Oh. Hey, Nick."

"Hey, Doanes. Give me some good news."

But, like his buddies door-to-dooring it on the second and third floors, the cop shook his head. "Sorry, man. I got nothing. Lots of empty apartments, and the few people who've answered didn't see anything, didn't hear anything, and mostly don't even know the people on their own floor, never mind one up. Merry said she was going to track down the super, though. Maybe she's got something better."

"I already talked to her. The super didn't recognize the vic's picture, said the apartment belongs to a woman, gave up her name and contact info. Merry got the renter on her cell phone—she was evasive, but eventually fessed up that she's out of the city on a training assignment, and advertised online for a sublet to offset the bills. Dennison said he'd only be here for a couple of weeks, but he paid her for a whole month. In cash."

"He was moving around, keeping a low profile like the others," Doanes observed.

"Seems like it." Question was, why? And why had he stayed in Bear Claw? What were the Investor and the other remaining members of the militia looking for? And why was the head honcho suddenly taking out his own people? What was going on here?

It felt as if they were chasing their own tails like a bunch of bomb dogs with C-4 strapped to their butts. Shaking his head, Nick continued, "Anyway, looks like the lady who rents the place is a dead end. She dealt with Dennison on the phone, never met him in person, didn't care what he was doing in town as long as he paid in full." He paused. "Are the CSIs still up there?"

Doanes shook his head. "I think they're done. I saw Gigi leaving a little while ago."

"Thanks." Nick waved him off. "Catch you later."

It shouldn't have mattered to him whether or not the analysts had finished up their preliminary run, just like it shouldn't have mattered that Jenn had been assigned to the scene. They had crossed paths plenty since the breakup, and had kept it friendly and polite. There shouldn't be any problem there. Hell, there *wasn't* any problem there.

Still, he breathed a little easier as he headed up the next flight of stairs, knowing he'd have the quiet solitude he needed to put himself into the head of Chuckie Dennison—a victim who had also been a killer in his own right. Nick wouldn't ever know the dead man personally, but for a few minutes—or longer, if necessary—he would do his damnedest to *become* him, standing in his space, seeing the things he'd thought were important, the things he hadn't.

Dennison had been a fugitive from both the law and his former boss…but he'd stayed in the city. What was keeping him here? And then the torture. What had the Investor wanted from his former lieutenant? Information, obviously, but what kind? What was the endgame here?

Nick probably wouldn't get the answers today, of course, but he would absorb everything he could of Dennison's space, his life, his death. And maybe—if he was damn lucky—get a flash of the kind that sometimes hit him, the sort of lightbulb *gotcha* that sent him in a new direction, or back down an old one, until he hit pay dirt. All because he'd stood there for ten minutes or an hour, absorbing every detail of a stranger's life and trying to figure out what made him tick.

The members of his sprawling, affectionate and high-drama family called it method acting and were as proud of his skills as they were baffled by his choices. His bosses were just glad he could do it, and used him as often as they could. And he was okay with that. More than okay with it. He came, he saw, he blended, he helped catch the bad guy and then he moved on again. That was his life, his skill set, and if it meant he'd put some other things on hold, better that than repeating past mistakes.

Now, as he pushed through the door to the fifth floor, he did his damnedest to put himself into the mind of a former member of the Ghost Militia, an ex-con who'd done a stint for aggravated assault and attempted murder, and who had been on the run, aware that the Investor was tracking down his former lieutenants and tearing them open to see what secrets he could find.

The hallway was identical to those on the other

floors, with white walls, a red carpet that was starting to go threadbare pink along the traffic pattern and numbered doors leading off on either side. The one difference was that the door on the far end was marked as a crime scene.

Already deep in Dennison's head—*I'm here, nobody followed me, gotta check the apartment first before I can relax, make sure I haven't been made yet*—Nick headed up the hall, senses attuned for the slightest warning of danger to his fugitive self.

Thud. The noise from behind the far door brought him up short and set off all sorts of warning bells—someone was in the apartment!

Where Dennison would've done a one-eighty and taken off, though, Nick powered straight ahead with his weapon appearing in his hand without him consciously reaching for it. It was probably one of the cops, he knew, but he wasn't taking any chances. Especially not when the others were supposed to be canvassing.

He went quiet as he got close to the door, moving almost silently on his lug-soled boots and letting out a breath as there was another *thudda-thudda-thud,* then a scuffle.

Instincts on overdrive, he twisted the knob, booted open the door and flattened himself against the outside wall for a second. When there was no response, he went in low, leading with his gun. "Freeze! Police!"

In the next moment, two impressions seared his retinas and competed for priority in his head: Jenn lay on the floor, motionless beside a battered chair, near a dark pool of blood he hoped to hell wasn't hers. And heavy footsteps coming from the back room said she wasn't alone.

Jenn! The word shouted in his head but didn't leave his lips. He reached her in two strides, went down on his knees before he knew it, and then had his hands on her for the first time in a month. Her pulse was fast, her breathing shallow, her eyes were closed, the side of her face already reddened and starting to swell. He didn't see any fresh blood, and the spatter nearby was old and set, but that didn't change the basic fact: someone had gone after her. And that someone was getting away.

He lunged to his feet, bellowing, "Stop! Police!"

Not that the guy stopped—they never did, and this one was already out the window. Nick knew it even as he cleared the door into the bedroom and heard the traffic, then the feet pounding down the fire escape. "Damn it!"

He stuck his head out, and just barely saw the guy from the back as he bolted around the corner onto the main road. But that was enough to relay the bad news— the guy had a pair of plastic boxes under one arm. He'd taken the evidence kits.

Cursing viciously, Nick holstered his weapon, went for his phone and called it in. But even with "white guy, six-something, dark pants and a suit jacket, carrying a couple of evidence kits" as a description, he didn't hold out much hope.

Given the head start, though, there was no point in Nick giving chase. Especially not when there was a vic who need medical attention.

Not a vic. Jenn. He had to think of her that way, though. It was the only way he could keep himself steady as he returned to Dennison's living room, went down beside her once more. He didn't move her, didn't dare do anything more than take her hand in his.

She was still unconscious, which wasn't good. And her left eye was nearly swollen shut, red and puffy. She'd taken a hell of a hit. Maybe more than one.

Anger was a sharp, ugly beast inside him, hammering against his ribs and snarling to be let free. He kept his control, though—that was what made him one of the best at what he did. But he sure as hell didn't feel like one of the best as he leaned over her. He felt damned helpless, and that was a new feeling.

"There's an ambulance on the way," he said, forcing his voice level. "They'll take care of you, get you back on your feet."

She would hate this, he knew. She would hate knowing that she'd been out of it, that she'd been the focus of an "officer down" call, taking attention away from the manhunt that even now was forming up down below. And most of all, she would hate knowing he'd been the one to wait with her.

Despite her professionalism, he knew the sharp edges were there, knew she couldn't possibly be as cool toward him as she came across. There had to be some heat beneath that mask, some anger over the way he'd ended things so abruptly when there'd been the potential for them to keep seeing each other, keep going with the crazy heat they'd made together.

Or maybe that was just him. Maybe she really was that cool, and he was the only one who still took a second some mornings to realize that she wasn't beside him, wouldn't ever be there again. "Come on, come on," he muttered, reaching for his phone. "Where the hell—"

Boot steps thudded in the hallway and Tucker straight-armed the door, face thunderous. "What the hell happened?" He missed a step at the sight of Jenn, down and out of it. He grabbed his radio and snapped, "Where the hell is that ambulance?"

"Three minutes out," came the muffled response from Dispatch.

"Get it here in one." Keeping the radio clutched, Tucker rounded on Nick. "Tell me." He sounded almost as mad as Nick felt. Almost.

"I came in as the dipwad was going out the window," Nick growled, and gave him a quick summary, along with his too-vague description of Jenn's attacker.

Tucker shook his head grimly. "This is bad."

"It gets worse. He got the evidence cases."

"He…" The detective broke into a string of curses, then headed for the hallway, already barking into his radio. "Anything on the guy Lang saw? Business suit, two plastic cases. Anything?"

His voice faded as he stalked down the hallway, giving orders and making threats that anyone who'd known him for more than five seconds knew was more a sign of how worried he was than anything. Tucker was no pushover, but he was a fair leader, and he cared deeply about all of his people. More, the crime scene analysts had a special place in his heart, given that his wife, the mother of his daughter, was one of them.

Nick didn't know what it meant to feel like that, to love like that. But he knew he was on the verge of losing it over Jenn.

In the distance, a siren throbbed faintly. *Finally!*

Tightening his fingers on hers, he leaned in. "They're almost here. Any minute now."

Her lashes fluttered.

"Jenn!" His muted shout sounded very loud in the room—in the freaking *murder* scene, the one he'd been

coming to re-create in his mind, only to wind up coming way too close to reenacting it in an entirely more gruesome fashion. There was nothing of Dennison in him now as he brushed a few strands of hair from her forehead. "That's it," he said, though she hadn't moved again. "Come on, baby. You can do it."

The "baby" just slipped out. But even as it resonated too deeply inside him, her fingers moved against his, her eyelids fluttered again and she inhaled a deep breath—a real one this time, not one of the shallow, shocky sips she'd been taking ever since his arrival.

And then, finally, she opened her eyes and looked up at him.

WARMTH RUSHED THROUGH Jenn at the sight of Nick's face so close to hers, and the knowledge that he'd been watching her sleep, and that whatever he'd been thinking, it had put deep, intense emotions in his eyes, making him look so fierce he was almost frightening.

Almost.

"Nick," she said softly, reaching for him. "What—"

She gasped when the move sent a slash of pain through her head, followed by a roll of nausea.

"Stay still." He gripped her hand. "You were attacked, knocked out. The paramedics are on their way up."

"Para...oh." She closed her eyes as her brain caught back up with her, and the scenery she had glimpsed behind Nick's head connected to her recent reality—or at least as much as it could when that reality was a jumble.

She was at a crime scene; there had been another torture-murder. She knew that much, though only as words, like Dispatch was reporting directly inside her head. In terms of really seeing things, really having the memories, the last thing she remembered was—*ow!* She moved to grab her head, then groaned when the motion made things worse. Grayness washed her vision and things went swimmy around her.

"Jenn!" Nick said urgently. "Come on, stay with me."

"You didn't want me to—" She had enough presence of mind to shut *that* off, clamping her lips together while she rode out a surge of nausea. Her mind raced, bringing more stabs of pain in her head and behind her eyeballs, but memories started coming back, too.

She remembered walking up the stairs to the fifth floor, coming in to find Gigi already working.

"Gigi!" Her eyes flew open and she tried to shove up off the floor, fighting through the pain and the too-bright glare of the winter sunlight and apartment fluorescents. "Where's Gigi? She was here!"

"Chill!" Nick gripped her shoulders, holding her down. "It's okay. You're okay. She's okay. She left on another call. You were here alone." He paused. "You don't remember her leaving?"

"I…" The fear had leveled off when she learned that Gigi was okay, but now it came back full force, roaring through her, sweeping through a jumble of memories. She remembered Gigi photographing the scene, the two of them talking about Nick. And after that…

What happened after that?

"Okay. It's okay. Don't stress about it. Just relax." But there was something in his eyes that she didn't like—it was too much like the looks she had gotten back in her old life, after Terry died and things started coming to light. It said, *There's more, and it's bad.*

"What is it?" she demanded, grabbing on to his

wrists and digging in, her heart suddenly pounding even harder. "What aren't you telling me?"

He hesitated, then said, "The bastard got your evidence kits."

"No!" Horror lashed through her. Shame. Guilt. The cases held everything from the scene. If it was all gone… She surged against him. "Let me up! I need to—"

"You need to stay the hell down!" he said fiercely, leaning in so their faces were very close and she could feel the heat of his body, his grip. But then a sudden clamor erupted at the door and two paramedics came in, puffing from the climb. At the interruption, Nick's expression flattened and he straightened away from her. "You need to let these guys have a look at you."

She tried to wave them off. "I'm fine." Which would've sounded more convincing if her voice hadn't broken. But she *wasn't* fine. She was down and hurting. And, worse, she had lost crucial evidence in the Death Stare case…otherwise, why else would the killer come back for it?

The killer, she thought, and closed her eyes as it started to penetrate. She'd been attacked, knocked out. Logic said that was what'd happened, but when she tried to remember, all she could picture was her and Gigi gossiping about Nick. Who was here, hovering over her with a gruff protectiveness he'd never shown while they were together, probably because she had been careful to never let him see her be anything but breezy and self-reliant. Now, she was anything but. She wanted to cling, wanted to cry. She had been attacked, knocked out, robbed.

Why couldn't she remember any of it?

The paramedics dumped their gear and moved in, asking questions and starting to tug at her clothes.

She tried to fend them off. "I don't—"

"Just let them have a look at you," Nick said. "You were unconscious for a good five minutes, and there's blood." She would've kept arguing, would've kept trying to brush them off when they tried to look in her eyes and feel the growing lump on her skull. But then he leaned in closer and said, "Please."

She stilled, caught in his eyes and the low-voiced request. Had he ever asked her for anything before? She didn't think so, and the impact was palpable. He was still holding her hand, she realized. He followed her eyes to where their fingers were twined together, but he didn't pull away. Instead, he tightened his grip.

Warmth kindled, making her want to lean into him, lean on him. Her head hurt; her eye and the whole side of her face hurt. More, her heart ached at knowing she had lost the evidence. Maybe even the key to the whole case.

Damn it. She needed to let go for a few minutes, needed to know she could trust someone else to handle things, needed… She needed exactly what he was offering right now, she realized with a sudden cold-water dose of reality. Which meant it wasn't real; it was just a means to an end, just like all the other roles she'd seen him play over the past month.

Stiffening, she pulled away, even though it took effort. "Whatever it takes to get the job done, right?"

He frowned. "What?"

"Never mind." Going numb now, she submitted to the paramedics, no longer trying to fight them off as they asked her to follow a pen with her eyes and answer stupid-simple questions about what day it was and who was the President.

Nick stood, moved to the back of the room and took a good look around. Moments later, he and Tucker had their heads together and were conferring in low tones, with lots of looks in her direction. She was so busy trying to focus on them that it took her too long to notice that the paramedic working on a small scalp laceration—which had started bleeding when she began to move around—was tossing bloody gauze into the spatter pattern from the murder vic.

"The scene," she protested, reaching for his arm. "Please!"

"Forget the scene," Tucker said, more to the paramedic than to her. "A living victim gets priority."

It was protocol, and normally she agreed wholeheartedly—the emergency responders needed to do their jobs without worrying about evidence. But she wasn't critical—a headache and some memory gaps weren't going to kill her—and this was the Death Stare case. "Not here. Not now. Not with me."

His expression darkened. "Stow it. You're damn lucky to be alive, you know. If Nick hadn't come in when he did, the bastard could have—" He broke off, cursing under his breath as he turned away to take a long look out the window.

Nick, though, didn't seem to have nearly as much of a problem with the prospect. He stared at her, expression unreadable and nothing like the gentleness that had been on his face when she was first waking up.

In a way, she was grateful, because the irritation she wanted to aim at him helped her steel herself against the picture Tucker had painted in her aching head. She hadn't thought about it, hadn't really questioned why or how Nick had gotten there. Now, though, she was forced to admit she was damned lucky to be alive. It wasn't like the Investor made a habit of leaving witnesses. Exactly the opposite, in fact.

Nick had interrupted him before he could finish the job. He had saved her life.

What was she supposed to do with that?

"Yes, I *am* lucky," she admitted, struggling to keep her voice from wavering. "I'm grateful Nick got here when he did, believe me. More grateful than I can really say right now. But that doesn't change the fact that I'm not seriously injured."

"You were unconscious for way too long," Nick said flatly, "and you're still out of it."

"I'm fine."

He raised an eyebrow. "Describe the attack."

She glared at him, but the reality was that she wasn't frustrated with him anymore—she was mad at herself. Why couldn't she remember what happened?

"You want the scene preserved? Then get out of here," Nick said with maddening logic. "Let the paramedics take you to the hospital for stitches and make sure that hard head of yours is fully intact." To Tucker, he said, "We'll want guards on her, starting now."

"Who did you have in mind?" The question seemed more pointed than it should've been, though Jenn couldn't be sure. Things were getting fuzzy all of a sudden, like a gray mist closing in on her.

"Send a couple of uniforms with her," Nick said flatly. "And have Alyssa or one of the others meet her there. I don't want... Hell, she should have a friendly face waiting."

Jenn didn't know why he sounded angry but couldn't worry about it just then, as the paramedics transferred her to the waiting stretcher. She moaned as the world around her began a big, sickening spin.

Nick took a couple of steps toward them. "Damn it, don't—"

"It's okay." She waved him off, gritting her teeth and forcing herself to cling to consciousness and not give in to the nausea. "I'm…I'm fine." Or she would be fine once she got out of here, got someplace dark and quiet, where she could be alone and process everything that had happened—and chill out enough to remember the rest. The memories had to be in there, they *had* to be.

She didn't know whether she had seen the Investor himself or one of his underlings, but it was an important break, a crucial turn in the case…if only she could remember what her attacker had looked like, what he had said. Had he asked her about the evidence? He must've come back for something specific, but what?

"Go on," Tucker said to the paramedics. To her, he added, "I'll have Alyssa meet you there. Gigi, too, if she's free."

"Thanks," she said softly. But it was Nick she reached out toward, though she didn't make contact. "Thank you for chasing him off. Lucky break or not, I owe you one."

"You don't owe me a damn thing." His expression was unreadable, his body utterly still. "I should've gone after him, should've caught him."

"I should be able to remember what he looks like. We don't always get what we want."

And he was exhibit A on that little fact of life, wasn't he? Because even with her woozy and concussed—or maybe because of those things—she was very aware of the imprint his body had left on hers, and the way her clothes now smelled slightly of him, a mix of new leather and his own uniquely masculine scent. She wanted to inhale him, remember him. But he wasn't the one she was supposed to be remembering, was he?

He had been the one to point out the memory gap to Tucker, but now he softened a little, saying gruffly, "Give it time. It'll come back."

BUT JENN'S MEMORY OF THE attack didn't come back. It didn't magically return that afternoon as she submitted to a battery of tests and grudgingly agreed to spend the night for observation, all too aware that there was a uniformed officer at the door. And it didn't come back later that night when she lay in the not-very-dark room, staring at the shadowy pieces of hospital equipment and trying to force the memories to return.

She remembered coming into the apartment and seeing the blood, the ropes, the chair, Gigi…then nothing. It wasn't even that she was fuzzy on the details, or her mind had been frozen in fear. She just didn't remember. Her world skipped from telling Gigi there wasn't anything between her and Nick anymore, and then waking up practically in his arms.

Unfortunately, every time she got to that part, she remembered all too well other times that she'd woken up in his arms. Then, when she deliberately steered her mind away from that, she skipped back to the attack, and how she owed him her life. If he hadn't walked into Dennison's apartment when he did, she'd probably be dead now. And that was a hell of a thought. As was knowing that she'd probably seen the Investor's face, making her a valuable witness…and possibly, as far as the killer was concerned, a loose end.

So it was no real surprise that she tossed and turned as if it was an Olympic sport and she was going for the gold, until the painkillers and her body's need to heal overrode her churning thoughts and she finally conked out.

She slept poorly and woke near dawn, but felt a heck of a lot better than she had. She could see out of her right eye and move without wanting to whimper or throw up, and that was a huge relief. Still, a few hours later when Tucker, Nick, Gigi and Maya all filed in past the uniformed guard, she could only shake her head, answering the question before it was asked. "No, I haven't remembered anything new. I'm sorry." Then, seeing their expressions—different mixes of anger and sympathy—she added, "And don't look at me like that. I'm fine. The doctors said so."

She didn't look fine, though. She'd seen herself in the mirror, bruised and battered, with a bandage at her hairline where they'd glued the gash shut rather than stitching it. And she'd seen Nick's wince when he'd first looked at her…and then looked away.

"Don't push yourself," Maya advised. "Post-concussion syndrome is nothing to mess around with. You might feel okay now, but if you overdo it you could set yourself back, or worse." Trim and petite in dark wool pants and a soft, creamy sweater, the exotic brunette could've been a model. She wasn't, though; she was the Bear Claw P.D.'s resident psych expert. Which made her Jenn's next best hope.

"Help me," she said, reaching out to her coworker from where she sat on the edge of the bed, wearing the yoga pants and hooded sweatshirt Gigi had brought from her apartment. "I don't care what it takes. Drugs, hypnosis, I'll do anything."

"You can do yourself a favor by not rushing things," Maya said. "We can try hypnosis later. For now, just relax."

"How can I?" She gestured to the window. The view of the parking lot wasn't terribly scenic, but beyond the cars rose the skyline of Bear Claw City, and beyond that the mountains. "He's out there killing people. I need to do whatever I can to help bring him down."

"Trust me, it's not worth killing yourself over this one case," Nick said bluntly. He didn't say *especially when it's not even your hometown.* She'd bet he was thinking it, though, given that he'd said similar things when they'd been together, as if to remind her that he was just passing through.

Should've listened. Now, though, she narrowed her eyes in his direction. "This is *the* case for Bear Claw, Detective. Hopefully there won't be another one like it here, ever. And I'm not trying to grandstand, here, I'm just trying to be part of the team."

His expression flattened. "You've earned your place. You don't need to keep earning it."

That hit close enough to make her wince, especially when he wasn't one of the ones who would be reviewing her probation…but Tucker was. "I'm not trying to impress anyone. I'm just trying to do my job."

"Which doesn't include you needing to solve the case single-handedly."

Jenn was sucking in a breath to retort when Tucker said mildly, "She's not trying to fling herself into the middle of a firefight, Lang, so dial it down." He cut a look at Jenn. "Both of you, take a breath and keep the personal stuff out of this, okay?" His tone was mild, but there was an undercurrent of steel, a subtle reminder that he was the boss here.

"But I wasn't..." She subsided, though, because Tucker had a point—she might've had the same debate with him or another of her teammates, but there wouldn't have been the same sort of emotion behind it: frustration, annoyance and the need to prove herself, not to her bosses, but to Nick.

Except that she was over him, damn it.

Letting out a sigh, she shook her head. "Sorry. You're right. I'll chill." And not just because her head was suddenly throbbing once more, her face gone sore and tender. "But I'm not backing off. I want to get these memories back and help get this guy, and his drugs, off the streets of *my* new city."

Besides, closing the case would mean that Nick would leave Bear Claw for good and she could get her mind back where it belonged—on the job, and eventually on finding a nice, uncomplicated guy for a nice, uncomplicated relationship with no manipulation, no heartbreak and no nasty surprises when she least expected them.

Chapter Four

To Jenn's intense frustration, it was two long weeks before she was cleared to put a foot inside the P.D. The doctors had wanted to play it safe with her concussion, and Tucker and the others hadn't trusted her when she promised to take it easy. As Gigi had put it, "Jenn has two speeds—on and more on. There's no way she's going to give herself enough recovery time unless we make her take it."

Jenn had been touched—if also irritated—by the way her coworkers-turned-friends had bundled her off to a safeguarded mountain retreat owned by two of the more elusive members of the Death Stare task force.

The getaway had come with state-of-the-art security and fortresslike reinforcements. That, along with a careful leak of details on her attack and inability to remember anything, had cocooned her away from the danger, while the safe house's amenities—hello ridiculously luxurious interior, stocked cabinets and king-size hot tub—had made her feel as if she was on a strange solo vacation.

She certainly hadn't been roughing it. If anything, she'd lived far better than she would have at home. More, she might even have to admit that the time alone, out in the middle of the woods, had given her some perspective on the situation in Bear Claw—not so much on the case, as there was only so much she could do on that front, but more on how she had handled things with Nick. Because that was the thing…she didn't need to handle things with him, not really.

He was just passing through, after all. And she was determined to stay put.

She loved the city, her job and her coworkers. She didn't just want to help solve the Death Stare case; she wanted to be a part of things in Bear Claw, not just now, but in the future, too. With Matt as the new mayor, determined to turn things around, the city was poised for some major positive changes. She wanted to be there when it happened. She wanted to make the city her new home, her new life.

Which meant she needed to not screw up during the last bit of her probationary period. She knew Tucker and the chief were happy with her work so far, but she didn't dare get complacent. Her gut said that the past could still come back to bite her in the butt somehow.

Which meant that, for all that she might have needed the not-quite-a-vacation in the woods—the bruises had faded and the cut had healed over to an angry red that would mellow in time—by the end of the second week, she was raring to go, packed and ready an hour before she was scheduled to be picked up.

She wanted to get back to work, wanted to prove herself, no matter what it took. There had been another murder, another torture victim. Not a lieutenant this time, but a cashier at a corner store, someone who didn't even have any apparent ties to the Ghost Militia.

Jenn knew one thing for certain, though: the Investor had to be stopped. And soon, before he found what he was looking for and left the area, only to begin again somewhere else, with a new city to terrorize.

To her relief, when the uniformed officers picked her up, they took her straight to the crime lab, where Maya was waiting for her, ready to try hypnosis if Jenn was on board.

Jenn's answer to that was a succinct "Hell, yes."

"I thought we should go back to Dennison's apartment. Sometimes revisiting the location can help bring things back."

Nerves jittered at the thought of returning to the scene, but Jenn nodded. "Sounds like a plan."

"Then, let's go." Maya climbed the stairs to the main floor. "I cleared it with Tucker this morning," the profiler said over her shoulder. "He said it was okay for us to use the apartment. Gigi and Alyssa have been through the scene a couple of times, but haven't really gotten any smoking-gun stuff. Which means you and I can go in there and see about jogging your memory without worrying about destroying evidence."

Jenn winced a little at the reminder of the potentially crucial evidence she'd lost, but nodded. "Thanks for setting it up ahead of time."

"We didn't think you'd want to ease into things."

"You were right about that." The time away had been good for her, but she hated that she still couldn't remember the attack, couldn't picture her attacker's face or recall what evidence she had packed away after Gigi left.

"Tucker insisted on us taking backup," Maya said as they hit the main floor, where doors led to the bullpen on one side, the main lobby on the other. Kelsey Meyers was at the front desk, dealing with the phone and keeping tabs on the waiting area. A crutch leaned up against the counter and her K9 partner, Amber, sat beside her.

The sight of the yellow Lab brought a twinge of memory, though not the kind Jenn was searching for. Nick had befriended Kelsey early during his stay in Bear Claw. He hadn't been flirting with her; no, he'd been drawn to Amber, wanting to know everything there was to know about working with a K9 partner.

When Jenn had suggested he should get a dog of his own, though, he just shook his head and said a guy like him couldn't have a responsibility like that, not when his work took him away for days at a time, sometimes weeks. Sometimes longer.

He'd given her plenty of warning, she had to admit. He couldn't have said it any louder if he'd hired a plane to write "This is only temporary" in puffy white vapor across the sky.

"An officer is going to meet us out by the car," Maya said as they headed for the parking lot. "Tucker said you're to stay in his sight at all times, and sound the alarm immediately if you see something suspicious, or even get a weird feeling on the back of your neck. Better safe than sorry."

Jenn nodded. "I'm not going to do anything stupid, like try to lose my bodyguard. Promise." She was still a potential witness—short-term memory loss could reverse at a moment's notice, after all.

They stepped through the door, into the secure area where the P.D. members parked their cruisers and personal vehicles. But then, as they approached Maya's dark green SUV, a figure straightened away from the bumper with a hands-in-pockets move that put Jenn on red alert and sent a surge of heat through her system—

one she wanted to believe was anger. *Nick*. She knew him by the way he moved, the way he looked at her, the way her body reacted.

She hadn't seen him for two weeks, hadn't thought she'd missed him. But the sight of the thick, raven-black hair brushing his shearling collar had her wanting to bury her fingers in it, and one look at his stern, uncompromising lips made her want to kiss him long and hard, until the planes of his face softened and his breathing came fast.

She wanted his body against hers, inside hers, pounding them both to oblivion, to a place where it didn't matter anymore that he'd dumped her or that she couldn't remember the Investor's face, it only mattered that they were there, together, riding each other blind, stupid and satisfied.

Even as her blood heated, she cursed him, then herself. Damn him for having been so good, for being there now. And damn her for not being able to let it go.

"What are you doing here?" she bit out as she and Maya got in range of the car, and the man.

"I'm going along to the Dennison place as your backup," he announced without preamble, without really looking at her. "Hope you don't mind." But his tone said it didn't matter if they minded or not, that was the way it was going to be.

NICK WAS BRACED FOR AN ARGUMENT, and didn't intend to lose. Now that Jenn was back in the city, with all the risk that involved, he intended to watch out for her, whether she liked it or not.

"I thought Tucker was going to assign a uniform."

A light flush stained her cheeks, hiding the dusting of freckles he'd once traced his fingers and lips across.

Wearing wool pants that outlined her curves and a clingy reddish-brown sweater that brought out the burnished highlights in her hair, she looked more like herself—the bruises had faded and the cuts had healed—yet there was a deep wariness in her eyes that hadn't been there before. He wasn't sure if it was because of him or the situation, or both.

"He changed his mind," Nick answered, not bothering to mention that he'd pretty much changed Tucker's mind for him, unwilling to leave her safety in somebody else's hands. Two weeks after the attack and he still flashed back on it, still kept thinking, "What if?" What if he'd been a few minutes later? What if her attacker hadn't bolted, but rather stayed to finish the job?

She set her jaw. "This isn't a good idea."

"He thinks it is. So do I." Usually, Nick wouldn't have tried to push himself in where he wasn't wanted, especially when it came to a woman. But the situation—and the woman—were far from his usual.

What was it about her that wouldn't let him walk away? She wasn't all that different from the other women he'd dated over the past six years, since his divorce. They were almost invariably career-minded, self-sufficient, sexy and independent. In other words, nothing like Stacia's blond vulnerability and home-and-hearth sensibilities, which had made her an incredible mother but a terrible match for an undercover cop.

There was some of that home-and-hearth in Jenn, too, though. She was tough and self-sufficient, yes, but the more he'd gotten to know her—not just during their time together, but also over the past month, when he hadn't been able to stop himself from watching her—the more he'd realized that she wasn't as much like him as he'd thought. She wasn't looking to work for a bit and then move on. She wanted roots, wanted a home base. A family.

He knew there was something in her past, some blot on her record she was trying to get away from—she'd hinted at it, and Tucker had volunteered to give him the whole story at one point. He'd turned down the offer, though, and hadn't given in to the low-grade temptation to look into the matter on his own. She was entitled to her secrets. God knew he had his own…and it wasn't as if they had been in that kind of relationship back then. Still weren't, which made it none of his business. Hell, *she* was none of his business.

Yet here he was.

To Maya, he said, "I wanted to take another look around the scene, anyway, and wouldn't mind bouncing my impressions off you for the psych perspective. And no offense to Tucker's uniforms, but I've got far more time in the trenches. I see things they don't. So I volunteered to play bodyguard."

The psych profiler pursed her lips but didn't argue. "You don't need to sell me on your qualifications… but I need to be sure that you won't interfere with the hypnosis."

"I won't make a sound," he promised.

"That wasn't what I was talking about. I need Jenn relaxed and concentrating on me, not you."

Damn. He hadn't thought about it like that. He'd been so focused on keeping her safe—and potentially getting his own look at her attacker if the bastard came back—that he'd lost track of the whole point of the exercise, and that he might jeopardize it.

Spreading his hands in what he hoped was a gesture of innocence, he said, "I just want to make sure you're safe, and get in a few minutes extra at the crime scene, that's all. If it'll help, I can wait out in the hall during the actual hypnosis."

But Jenn looked away and shrugged. "That won't be necessary. Sit in, don't sit in, your call." She might as well have said, *I don't care what you do.* Certainly implied it.

He hadn't meant it as a challenge, but that was how she'd taken it. That probably should've brought a wince, maybe even made him back down. Instead, he nodded. "Then I'll sit in. Thanks."

He didn't think he'd just played her, certainly hadn't meant to. Sometimes it just came as second nature, though.

They rode to the Dennison apartment in silence and without any evidence of a tail, and parked close to where he'd lost sight of Jenn's attacker. It had been a couple of weeks, but part of him still wanted to duck around that corner and have another look, try to put himself inside the Investor's head. It wouldn't do him any good, though. He'd tried it already—more than once—but just couldn't get inside the bastard's mind. He knew all the details of the case, knew the kind of man they were dealing with—smart, meticulous, ambitious, already powerful and seeking more—and what that sort was likely to think and do…but the Investor's actions didn't fit the pattern, which had Nick off his game.

Normally, a guy like this would've left town right before the militia went down. Or if not then, right after.

He would've cut his losses, found a new city and started over. Someone this careful, this meticulous, normally wouldn't have stayed put, and he certainly wouldn't have gone on a killing spree when there hadn't been any evidence before that he'd done any of the actual killing.

The Investor, though, had stuck. Was still sticking. And according to the word on the street—and Nick's gut instinct—he was doing the killing. *Where are you, you bastard? What are you up to? What do you want?*

"You coming?" Jenn asked coolly, making him aware that he'd paused on the sidewalk, out in the open.

"Yeah. I've got your back." And, damn it, he needed to make sure of that. *Focus.*

He kept his senses maxed as they headed upstairs, but he didn't see anything out of place. The carpet was the same, the stairwell had the same echo and, when he popped his head into the second-floor hallway, one of the residents gave him the same semi-bored look the cops had gotten before, with even less interest now because of the police presence over the past couple of weeks.

When they reached the apartment, he went in first and took a quick look around before returning for the women. He stepped back out into the hallway, saying, "It's clear." Maybe too clear.

The apartment had been stripped, cleaned and repainted, the floors refinished, and it didn't look anything like it had before. The bones were the same, but the space echoed now, and smelled of paint, sawdust and polyurethane. He questioned whether it would trigger any of the memories Jenn and Maya were hoping for. It sure as hell wasn't giving him anything to work with when it came to getting inside Dennison's head, or the Investor's.

Maya went in first. When Jenn slipped past him, he said quietly, "Last chance. I'll wait in the hall if you'd rather."

She hesitated, but then shook her head. "You should be in here with us. If I start remembering, who better to ask the questions?" Her lips twisted in a bitter-seeming smile. "You're one of the best interrogators I've seen."

Her expression made him wonder what she'd seen, and why. He didn't ask, though, wasn't sure he wanted to know. So instead, he said, "You're not a suspect."

"But I'm a witness. Or at least I should be. Fingers crossed." She entered the apartment, leaving the door open behind her.

Nick hesitated. Was she testing herself or him? Or did she really not care if he was in the room? Maybe she didn't, he acknowledged. Maybe he was the only one who was having trouble moving on from a relationship—an affair, he corrected, not a relationship—that he'd been the one to end.

So he followed her in, hoping this wasn't a mistake.

In the absence of furniture—or anything, really—the women sat cross-legged on the floor, right near where the bloodstains had been sanded away, the floor refinished. Not letting himself picture Jenn lying sprawled in that same spot, motionless and bloodied, Nick wandered to the bedroom and glared out the window, toward where her assailant had disappeared.

Behind him, Maya spoke softly, telling Jenn to relax and count her heartbeat, her breaths, and picture a happy place. And while Nick wasn't about to volunteer for hypnosis—he didn't want anyone crawling inside his head, thanks—he found himself breathing along with them, maybe even relaxing a little.

Letting out a sigh, he headed back to the main room and paused in the doorway. Jenn had her back to him, sitting cross-legged with her hands on her knees, in a compact fold that made him think he could scoop her up one-handed and toss her, laughing, over his shoulder to carry her to bed. Only he couldn't. Not anymore.

And he needed to get the idea—and the woman—out of his head, except in a professional capacity. He was her bodyguard right now, nothing more and nothing less.

"You're in this room," Maya said quietly, "only it's not empty anymore. What do you see?"

Jenn hesitated for a moment, but then said slowly, "There's blood spatter around a chair. Ropes. Kitchen knives. And the smell." Her voice sharpened on the last word. "God, I hate that smell, hate seeing things like this. Gigi's here, though. She knows I can't stand this part. So she's talking to me, making it a little easier."

He hadn't known crime scenes got to her, never would have guessed from seeing her working them. The detail shouldn't have tugged at him. If anything, it should've made him want to back off even further than he already had—he didn't go for vulnerability, after all.

"Okay, good," Maya said. "That's good. But Gigi gets a call. She needs to leave."

Jenn nodded. "I tell her it's fine, I don't mind finishing up."

"Then what happens?"

"Then…" Jenn's expression clouded. "Then Nick is there, looking down at me. Why is he there? Why is he staring at me like that?"

He shifted a little against the door frame, not sure what she'd seen in him.

"It's okay, you're okay." Maya shot him a raised eyebrow, but said only, "Let's back up a little. Gigi is still there. She's leaving, though, heading off on the other call. You tell her that you'll take all the case evidence back with you.... What happens next?"

Jenn frowned, but then her expression smoothed out. "She makes me promise to get one of the officers to help me carry everything, then she leaves and I keep working."

Nick tensed and shared a quick glance with Maya. This was new. Always before when Jenn had tried to talk about the attack, her memories had stopped before Gigi left the room.

Granted, it had been long enough, and hypnosis was inexact enough, that they could be dealing with false memories she had unknowingly created to fill in the crucial gaps. He was willing to take that chance, though; they all were. They would take just about anything if it had even a chance of producing a new lead in the Death Stare investigation. With the murder of the store clerk and two more overdoses in the past week, the death toll was still on the rise. This had to stop, now.

"Okay, so you keep working after Gigi leaves," Maya confirmed. "What evidence do you collect?"

They had been through the list of samples that Gigi and Jenn remembered collecting, and nothing had jumped out as a potential smoking gun, something important enough that it would've been worth the killer coming back for. Which meant that either it had been something routine that the Investor had been worried about, something the analysts hadn't seen that he'd taken away when he left the apartment the second time...or it was something Jenn had found after Gigi left.

"I finish up in the main room and start in the bedroom. There's a pair of boots in the corner with soil in the treads. Maybe that'll help."

Maya's eyebrows rose and she glanced at Nick, but he shook his head and said quietly, "Alyssa collected the boots after Jenn's attack. Compared to the original crime scene photos, it didn't look like they'd been touched."

She nodded. "What happens after you notice the boots?"

"Someone comes in." Jenn straightened and looked toward the apartment door. "Gigi must've sent one of the officers—" Her face blanked, but not with terror. It was more the confusion of someone coming awake. She blinked a couple of times. "Nick's here. What's he doing here? Why is he looking at me like that?"

"Damn," Maya muttered under her breath. She sent him a sidelong look and shook her head. "That may be all we get."

"You took her further than she'd been going before. Keep trying."

She did, but it didn't work. Even under careful questioning, Jenn's memories kept skipping from looking at the boots to seeing Nick as she regained consciousness. The intervening minutes were gone.

It took Maya a few minutes to bring her back around and brief her on the results—or lack thereof.

Jenn shook her head and winced a little, pressing her fingers to her temples. "Well. That was a big waste."

"It was worth a try," Maya said, but didn't argue that it had been a failure.

"Come on." Nick held out a hand. "Let's get you back to the P.D." If they weren't getting anywhere, he wanted her safely behind reinforced concrete and a full shift of cops.

She hesitated, but then let him help her up off the floor. She tugged her hand away almost immediately, though, and didn't look at him as she headed for the door.

Which was just as well, he told himself. Given that he was suddenly having a hard time remembering to keep his damn distance, he should count himself lucky that she wasn't having any such trouble.

A phone rang, interrupting the moment, which was probably also a good thing.

Maya pulled her cell from her pocket, and answered, "Maya here." Her brows furrowed slightly. "Hold on." Lowering the phone, she said, "I'm going to need a few minutes."

He nodded. "We'll wait in the hallway."

"No, go on down to the car." She tossed him the keys. "I'll be right with you."

He hesitated, but there was no real reason for him to hover. "Okay," he said after a brief pause. "We'll see you down there."

He and Jenn headed out into the hallway and down the stairs, and as she determinedly ignored him and the air went tense and tight between them, he realized too late that Maya had been a necessary buffer. Now, with the two of them alone, he was sorely tempted to crowd close enough that their arms bumped, close enough that he could feel her soft warmth and know that she was truly okay.

Except he'd given up the right to touch her the day he'd moved out of her apartment with what he now admitted—inwardly, at least—had been a really lame explanation, and a crummy way to treat someone he had cared about far more than he'd wanted to admit. So he kept his distance instead.

Down on the street level, he took a quick scan of their surroundings and a look under the SUV, then waved Jenn toward the car. "It's clear. Come on."

But then, just as she stepped out into the road and headed for the passenger side, an engine revved and a small, dark hatchback flew around the corner and accelerated further, aiming straight for her.

"Jenn!" Nick launched himself into the street, going for her, for the car, for whatever he could reach in time. But even as he bolted for his protectee—for *Jenn,* damn it—he knew the terrible truth.

In keeping his distance for his own protection, he was too far away for hers. And now he was going to be too late.

Chapter Five

Jenn started to flatten herself against the SUV, but when the small car corrected to follow the move, shock rattled through her. The driver was coming straight for her!

"Jump!" Nick shouted, sounding far away. "Get on the roof!"

Adrenaline spurted as she grabbed the roof rack and made an awkward lunge for the top of Maya's SUV.

It was a long way up, taller than she could manage with a flat-footed leap, which left her scrambling, trying to haul herself up as the car hit the back corner of the SUV. Metal screeched and tore as the smaller car kept going, plowing along the side of Maya's car, straight for Jenn.

"I've got you!" Strong hands grabbed her wrists and pulled.

Jenn's eyes snapped up to meet Nick's as he dragged her up to the top of the SUV, his eyes hard and wild. He pulled her all the way up, bracketed her with his arms and held her as the screeching, scraping continued and the vehicle rocked and shuddered beneath them.

Then the little car tore away and accelerated down the street, its engine howling and metal scraping on metal where its bumper was bent and dangling.

The hatchback screeched around the next corner and disappeared, leaving a loud silence that hammered in Jenn's head and rasped in her lungs as panic caught up with her. *Oh, no,* she thought. *That didn't just happen. Oh, no. Oh, no. No, no, nonono...*

All that made it out of her, though, was a low moan.

"Come on." Nick dragged her off the other side, down to the curb, and pulled her into a stumbling run. "We need to get you inside. Now!"

Suddenly the building seemed very tall and menacing, the crossroads at either corner a source of fear. Jenn's heart pounded sickly in her chest. Someone had tried to run her down! What if there was a shooter out there, a bomber, another car?

Even though her logical self knew the Investor wouldn't have bothered having her run down if he'd had a sniper in place, she didn't breathe again until they were inside the apartment building, with her in a corner near the stairs, Nick's body between her and the door as he yanked out his phone and called it in.

She hadn't screamed, she realized with that odd sort of clarity that comes after a near-disaster. She hadn't had time to scream or even really be afraid—it was over that fast. Now, though, she was very aware of the sharp skitter of panic in her veins and the warm solidity of Nick's body between her and danger.

"Black Honda hatchback, Colorado plates." He rattled off the information and a brief description of the driver, neither of which she had gotten. Then he ended the transmission and shoved the phone back in his pocket. But where she might've thought he would head for the door, maybe even take off after the guy, he turned back to her, eyes dark and almost wild. "Are you okay?"

"I'm…" She nearly took a step back away from him, not sure how to interpret the sudden intensity in his face, the sudden sense that he was utterly present, entirely focused on her. "Jenn!" he snapped, gripping her arms with granite gentleness. "Are you hurt?"

She shook her head, unable to speak over the race of blood through her veins, the thunder of her pulse. Part of her wanted to know what his angle was, what he was trying to get her to think or feel. But another part said, *This isn't a role. This is him.* His expression was raw, his eyes those of the man she'd thought she knew. One who was worried about her, who cared for her.

He gripped her arms. "Are you sure? Answer me, damn it."

The press of his fingers wasn't painful so much as insistent, solid and very real. "I'm…I'm fine. He didn't get me."

"Are you sure?" He shifted his grip, started patting her down. "Are you bleeding?"

"I said I'm fine." She caught his hands, held them hard when he would have pulled away. "Nick. I'm okay." Then, as he stilled—as they both stilled—she became very aware that they were alone in the stairwell, standing pressed together with their fingers intertwined. "I'm okay," she repeated, seeing it finally getting through. And, more, as it got through to her that he had saved her life once more. "I'm fine, thanks to you," she said softly. "If you hadn't been there, I wouldn't have made it onto the roof of that car. I would have…" She trailed off, not wanting to say it.

He scowled, eyes darkening to storms. "Damn it, Jenn."

"What? It wasn't my—"

He moved in. And kissed her.

SOMEWHERE IN THE BACK OF Nick's brain, he knew he was losing it, had already lost it. They were in the middle of a situation. But that was exactly why it had to happen now. Not later. Not when there might not have *been* a later.

It made him crazy to think that if he'd been a split second later, if she hadn't managed to jump rather than trying to escape on ground level, he wouldn't be holding her warm, living, breathing body now. Best-case scenario, he'd be huddled over her in the street, praying for the ambulance to get there fast enough. Worst case...

He tightened his grip on her and held on to a kiss that he didn't have any real right to take, but couldn't stop himself from needing like he needed his next damn breath.

After a first startled noise, she held herself stiff and still against him, with her hands curled around his wrists, not pushing him away, but not pulling him close, either. Her lips were closed, her body an arc of silent protest, not saying *stop it* so much as *what the heck?*

"I know," he said against her lips. "This is nuts. You should push me away, call me a bastard, tell me I don't get to dump you but still want you this way." She was going to have to be the one to bring them back to reality, because in that moment, with the threat of losing her too damn close to the surface, he couldn't be rational anymore.

Her hands went to his collar and dug in, holding him

close for a second. Then she shoved him back—not far, but far enough so they were looking in each other's eyes and breathing each other's breaths. "You still want me."

It wasn't a question, but he answered, anyway. "I don't play games. Not like this."

He didn't know why that put new shadows in her eyes, didn't know why she drew away a little more. And—bastard that he was—he didn't care. He closed on her, blood riding high from the taste of her on his lips and the feel of her hands on his collar, gripping as if she wanted to drag him closer but couldn't let herself give in to the urge.

She didn't trust him, and he didn't blame her, not after what he'd done, the way he'd ended things between them. But what she didn't get was that he'd been trying to do the right thing before. Now, though, he couldn't find it inside himself to do the right thing anymore. He was stripped down, flayed bare by the sight of her trying to get out of the way of the oncoming car. Hell, by having spent the past two weeks knowing she was safe yet still wanting—needing—to see it for himself.

He was about to drag her closer, about to show her the things he damn well couldn't say aloud, when her eyes changed, going suddenly hot and hungry as she gave in to the race of adrenaline and the heat that was building between them.

Her mouth shaped his name, and her fingers went from holding him away to finally pulling him close. Then she hesitated and, with their lips just a breath apart, she whispered against his skin, "You'd better not be playing with me this time, Lang. You do that, and you'll regret it."

That probably should've sent him off rather than

turning him on, probably should've had him backpedaling at warp speed.

Instead, he closed the final distance between them and kissed her for real.

Her lips were warm and soft beneath his, her fingers tight on his collar, pulling him close once more. He lingered there for a few thuds of his heartbeat, kissing only her lips, and then easing between them to take her tongue with his.

She gasped, letting him in deeper, and shifted restlessly against him until their bodies aligned through their winter clothes, warm and yielding. Her hands went to his shoulders, his nape, and then she was wrapping her arms around him, leaning on him, murmuring against his mouth.

Groaning, he touched her the way he'd wanted to for so long, burying one hand in her thick, silky hair while the other stroked along her spine, down to her curved buttocks and back up again. Heat surrounded him, suffused him, and he reveled in it as he kissed her again and again, wringing a sexy, throaty whimper from the back of her throat as he changed the angle, the depth, and locked his knees when his head went light.

This. This was what he'd had, what he'd pushed away. What he'd tortured himself with wanting.

She was sweet and vibrant in his arms, with a brilliant energy that poured into him, bringing a crazy mix of lust, joy and hope, all of which had been in damn short supply in his life lately. She was the opposite of the darkness he usually worked under, an antidote to the numb detachment that kept him sane and alive.

She made him feel alive, though, and sane. Centered.

Like he could do anything, *be* anything, even a normal guy having a normal fling.

He broke the kiss, whispered her name and trailed his lips along her cheek and across her throat, where her pulse throbbed hard and fast. "You're okay," he said against her skin, finally beginning to believe it. "I got you. You're okay."

Where before she would have said something about having herself and not needing him to take care of her, now she let her head fall back on a moan, giving him better access to her throat, the hollow between her collarbones, the soft skin of her earlobes. He caught one of her studded earrings in his mouth and suckled gently, wringing another moan. Her hands slipped to his shoulders, his chest, and she went pliant against him, lost, like him, in the moment and the heat.

Overhead, a door suddenly slammed in the stairwell, followed seconds later by a clatter of footsteps punctuated by an agitated call. "Jenn! Where are you? What happened?"

Maya!

Nick froze as his adrenal gland dumped a fresh load of "what the hell are you doing?" into his system and his heart slammed into a new gear, one that had a deep disquiet warring with the part of himself that wanted to keep kissing her, wanted Maya to see them together.

Jenn reacted a split second before he did, tearing her lips free and levering him away. "Oh, no!" Her face wasn't pale anymore, but the quick flush of color didn't do a thing to conceal the just-kissed look of her lips and the wide dreaminess of her eyes. Those eyes sharpened fast, though, going to near panic. "Don't let her know!"

Her knee-jerk instinct stung more than it should

have. And even as he was dealing with that—and the part of him that wanted to tuck her right back into that corner, cover her with his body and lose himself in another kiss that claimed her, possessed her—he was going into damage control mode.

It'd saved his life countless times undercover; it would buy them time now, even though he wasn't sure he wanted it.

She did, though, and he would give it to her. She deserved that and more from him.

Grateful for the bulky winter jacket that covered his raging erection, he swung around to face the stairs, putting his back to Jenn, blocking her in safely. "She's here," he called as Maya pounded down to the nearest landing. "She's okay."

She stumbled to a halt, wide-eyed and panting, with her phone clutched in her hand. "I heard from Dispatch. What in God's name happened?"

"The bastard was waiting for her," he said flatly. "I checked the SUV for wires, but he went old-school. Assault with a deadly hatchback."

Maya's eyes went beyond him. "You could've been killed!"

"Nick got me out of harm's way." Jenn nudged him aside to go to her friend. "I'm fine. Just a little shaken up, that's all. Your SUV is going to need some work, though."

"Forget the car. You're what's important." To Nick, Maya said fervently, "Thank you. If you hadn't been there…"

He nodded and said the right things, but as his system started to level off and his logical self came back to the fore, he was all too aware that they'd gotten damn lucky just now. He hadn't been paying enough attention. He'd let himself get distracted, trying to talk himself out of exactly what he'd just done.

Scowling, he cursed under his breath.

Jenn turned back. "What's wrong?"

Everything. Nothing. Damn it. He didn't know how to answer that, didn't know how to deal with the hot possessiveness that was still pumping in his veins, making him want to drag her back into his arms and surround her, protect her.

One of the reasons he was so good at his job was his ability to stay detached in even the worst situations. It wasn't that he didn't feel the emotions—he did, and deeply—but always before he'd been able to distance himself enough to do his job.

Granted, this wasn't an undercover assignment and Jenn wasn't a suspect he needed to question or an asset he needed to turn. But that only made it harder for him to turn away from where she and Maya were talking in low tones, with lots of reassuring touches and exclamations.

Distance. He needed some damn distance.

Sirens and tire chirps outside heralded the arrival of their reinforcements, which should've been a relief. Instead, Nick wanted to bare his teeth and bristle as Tucker came through the door. Which wasn't rational, he knew. *He* wasn't rational.

Because of that, and because he knew he'd made a grave mistake just now in kissing Jenn, he turned away from her, jerking his head for Tucker to follow so they could debrief in relative private. He was aware of her eyes following him over to the other side of the stairwell, aware of her expression going from confusion to anger. And he told himself it was for the best. Better to have her mad at him than trying to be a hero.

Angry was better than dead any day.

THE NEXT COUPLE OF HOURS were a blur, as Jenn found herself hustled back to the P.D. and down into the crime lab, which now had officers posted at the front and rear staircases. More, she found herself the target of half-hour check-ins by Tucker or one of the other detectives, whose "Hey, how's it going down here? Need anything?" queries were code for *Hey, we're just making sure you're still down here, and nobody's gotten to you yet*.

And that was a hell of a thought.

Where before the lab had been her safe haven, the place where she could hunker down away from the violence of the crime scenes and do the work she was truly good at, now she was trapped there. Worse, she was risking the sanctity of the lab by being there. If the Investor made it past the guards—a chilling thought but one she couldn't banish from her racing brain—she wouldn't be the only casualty.

What if one of the others was down there with her, working on her own evidence, like Gigi was now? As much as Jenn wanted to stay safe herself, she didn't want to do it at the expense of a coworker, a friend.

More, even if there wasn't any human collateral damage, the Investor had already shown that he knew enough to tamper with evidence. Who knew what he might do to the lab. More, just having him down there could taint the chain of custody…and she knew firsthand how much damage something like that could do, not just to the department, but to all the criminal cases whose evidence was housed in the basement lab. There had to be hundreds of them, thousands.

All in jeopardy because of her.

Thoughts whirling up to pressure-cooker steam, she shoved away from her desk and looked around, not really seeing the basement fortress, with its too-bright lights and determinedly cheerful posters. "I need to get out of here."

"Over my dead body," Gigi said from her desk, without taking her eyes off her computer screen.

Jenn shuddered. "It might come to that. Which is why I should go."

"Go where?"

"I don't know. Back to the safe house, maybe." She hadn't even realized she was thinking it until the words came out. But the appeal was undeniable. Up at the mountain retreat, she hadn't needed to worry about the people around her, the evidence, or even really her own safety. She had been protected. Inviolate.

Or had that been an illusion, too?

Gigi glanced over, frowning uncertainly. "If that's really what you want, it could probably be arranged."

"No." Jenn exhaled heavily. "It was nice while it lasted, but by the end I was going nuts wanting to be back down here, in the middle of the case. This is me." She gestured around the lab. "This is how I can help. Not by hiding out up in the woods in somebody else's love nest."

Unfortunately, the thought of the huge hot tub, padded floor and gas fireplace—complete with a fake bearskin rug so cheesy it was wonderful—made her think of something else. Or, rather, some*one* else…and a kiss.

Granted, she could tell herself it had been a combination of relief and adrenaline on both their parts, as well as a need to cling to something safe and solid on hers. More, she had needed to remind herself that she was still alive, even though the Investor wanted her dead.

It was a terrifying thought, and could've excused the kiss.

Or it would have, if it hadn't been for what he'd said about still wanting her, and being a bastard for acting the way he had. The look in his eyes and the fervency of his kiss had said he was telling the truth. And there had been no hiding her response. Not then and not now.

Which left them…where? She didn't know, and it wasn't as if they'd had any time to talk about it. Heck, she wasn't even sure he *wanted* to rehash it all.

Over the past six weeks, she had talked herself out of caring for him, out of wanting to be near him, be with him…at least she thought she had. One kiss, though, and she was right back where she'd started—wanting him and ready to damn the consequences, even when she knew that was a really bad idea.

Her hormones apparently didn't care about the possibility—the certainty—of disaster. They just wanted the man.

"So if you don't want to hide out—and I didn't think you would—then you should darn well stay here and do your job," Gigi said pragmatically. "And trust the rest of us to do ours, which includes protecting you."

That wasn't an empty boast, either. While most of the analysts were lab rats with some field experience, Gigi had completed all the training to be a technical specialist with a big-city SWAT team, and had only turned down the position they'd offered her because she'd opted to stay in Bear Claw with Matt when he became acting mayor. She was still licensed to carry concealed, though, and could strategize, shoot or fight her way out of most any situation.

"Don't tell me you're on babysitting duty, too?" Jenn probably should've guessed. It just went to show how wrapped up she was in her own head that she hadn't seen it.

"We just want to make sure you're safe."

"I appreciate it. Please don't think I don't know what you're doing for me, what everyone is doing for me here." She was the new kid on the block, and although she was working her butt off, she hadn't really contributed all that much to the most important cases. Yet somehow she'd wound up with some of the P.D.'s top people treating her like a key member of the team.

It was such a sharp contrast from how things had gone at her last job that she still kept waiting for it to all fall apart.

"But…?" Gigi prompted.

"Is it worth it? The manpower, I mean. The guards, the time away, all of it. I know when Tucker first sent me to the safe house, we were all hoping I'd be able to remember exactly what happened to me up in Dennison's apartment."

"Nobody's expecting a miracle, Jenn. It's not up to you to solve this single-handedly."

"I realize that, I do…intellectually, anyway. Emotionally, though, I hate that I failed at the hypnosis."

"The technique failed, not you."

"Still, it really stinks knowing that the key to cracking the Death Stare case once and for all could very well be locked up here." She tapped her temple. "And

I can't get it out. That's almost worse than knowing I lost the key evidence."

She had been in the same room with something the Investor had feared enough to come back for. She might even have held it in her gloved hands. It was gone now, though, and the evidence the Investor had left behind— including the boots she was working on right now, with their soil-clogged treads—wasn't giving them what they needed. At all.

"It wasn't your fault that he took the evidence. Hello, you were unconscious. Besides, if you're going to blame yourself, then I should feel guilty for leaving you alone at the scene."

"That's stupid."

Gigi just looked over with a raised eyebrow. *Well?*

Ignoring that, Jenn kept going. "What if I hadn't assumed it was one of the cops? What if I had been more on my toes when he first came into the apartment? What if I'd managed to call for help?"

"Then you'd probably be dead," Gigi said flatly. "Because there's no way he would've just knocked you out and then searched the apartment for whatever he'd come back for. He would've gone into the kitchen, found whatever weapons he'd left behind the first time, and he would've finished you off."

That brought a shiver and a sick surge of bile, but Jenn forced it down and shook her head. "I can't think like that. I can't live like that. Not if I'm going to do my job."

Her friend's expression softened. "What's really going on here, Jenn? Are you afraid this is going to look bad when your probationary period is up? Because if that's the case, I don't think you should be worried.

You're doing the job. You fit in here and you're damn good at what you do."

"No, it's not that." Or not entirely. "It's *this*." She glared at her computer screen, which was showing enlarged images of granular brown soil particles. "The evidence." She waved into the other room, where the boots were locked up, bagged and tagged. "The case. All of it."

"Hey," Gigi said softly. "Nobody's expecting a miracle—we're just treating you like part of the team, which you are. You don't have to push yourself to do anything more than your best as an analyst, and there's no question that you're doing exactly that. So chill." She slanted Jenn a pointed look. "Unless, of course, your frustration isn't really about the case. Say, maybe, it's more about something else?"

Jenn flushed. "I thought Maya was our resident shrink."

Gigi's grin turned wicked. "She's been known to blab, especially when it's not something bound by any kind of doctor-patient confidentiality. Like something she might've seen in a certain stairwell."

"It was nothing, really." But the flush climbed higher.

"That wasn't how Maya saw it."

"I can't *let* it be anything," Jenn corrected herself. Learning that he still wanted her shouldn't change anything between them, really. It didn't make up for him having dumped her without any real explanation, and it didn't change the kind of guy he'd turned out to be.

"Why not?"

"Because it's over." Except for that kiss. "It wasn't ever anything serious." Which was technically true.

"If you say so," Gigi said dubiously, but then turned

back to her computer screen. Jenn let out a breath, grateful for the reprieve. She was just looking back at the soil samples, which had sedimented to different levels in the liquid-suspension test she'd run, when Gigi said, "Matt and I weren't supposed to be serious, you know."

Jenn stilled, staring at the soil layers without really seeing them anymore. "Yeah. I know. He told me." She had been surprised to hear that the former SWAT leader had fallen for a cop, even more surprised to learn that he'd taken over the mayor's office in Bear Claw. He'd never been a joiner. When she'd gotten to know Gigi, though, she had understood. And she had enjoyed Matt's story about how the two of them had met—the flamboyant city-girl analyst butting heads with the reserved head ranger, and the two of them fighting their chemistry because she hadn't had any intention of sticking around Bear Claw City for long.

They had made it work in the end, Jenn knew. But that didn't mean that it would work for her and Nick.

Gigi flashed a quick grin. "I thought he might have told you about it. I've stopped being surprised to discover that the original loner had a friend or two back in his previous life."

"We were only ever friends, nothing more," Jenn said quickly, not sure if there was a question implied there. "He helped me get through a really bad time in my life."

"Yeah. I know. He told me what happened back at your old crime lab."

Jenn exhaled, relieved both by her friend's easy acceptance of her and Matt's past, and by not having to tell her the whole sordid story. "So you understand why I need to focus on keeping my job. Eighteen months of working in a paternity testing lab was more than enough." Her gesture encompassed the basement crime lab, with its high-tech equipment and evidence lockers. "This is what I want to do, who I want to be."

"And you think being involved with Nick would jeopardize that?"

"It doesn't matter, really. I'm not interested in starting back up with a guy who dumped me with zero explanation the moment things started to get a little complicated. That wasn't a cool move, and I'm not putting myself in that line of fire a second time."

"What if he made a mistake?"

Jenn started to give a "whatever" answer, but then found herself pushing away from the soil samples to turn and face her friend fully. "Even if he did, even if he apologized and asked for a second chance, I don't know that I would go for it. I've had time to step back and really look at him, and I'm not sure he's the guy I fell for. Besides, he's going to be gone as soon as this case is over with, and I want to stay here. You and Matt might've found a compromise that worked for you, but you're the exception, not the rule. Given all that, what's the point of starting up again when it's only going to end sooner than later?"

"The point is that it'd be fun while it lasted." Gigi blinked at her innocently. "Wasn't that what you said the first time around?"

"Oh, shut up." Trapped in her own logic, Jenn spun back around to glare at her samples. "That's just cr—"

She broke off, thinking, *Why, yes, it* is *crap.* Not what Gigi had been saying—though, that was garbage, too—but the sample itself.

Manure-laced soil, to be exact, along with some

grains and a bit of what she thought might be hay chaff. "Hey," she said, surprised. "Take a look at this."

Gigi rolled over and stared at the layers while Jenn explained, but after a moment, she shook her head. "You're the expert here. If you say it's cow poop, I believe you." She paused. "And if you tell me to be excited, I will be. I'm not sure why, though, given that there are a *lot* of cows outside of the city."

Bear Claw might be famous for its ski slopes and state forest, but a good chunk of the surrounding flatlands were straight out of the Old West. Some of the spreads were still working ranches that maintained huge herds of beef cattle, while others had gone in different directions to combat the tightening economy, ranging from crops, to ostrich and buffalo farming, to becoming guest ranches with guided trail rides and gourmet meals. And, inevitably, others had failed altogether and now lay fallow and dispirited.

"It's a long shot that I'll be able to identify exactly where Dennison's boots picked up this dirt," Jenn admitted, "but here's the thing. I've taken samples from a number of the area ranches, and I can get more. Which means I can run some comparisons. Failing that, if it's commercial feed, I might be able to match the grain and see who in the area uses it." What was more, she had an excited flutter in the pit of her stomach. It wasn't quite an *aha* moment, but it was more than they'd gotten from the other scenes.

Gigi whistled. "Okay, now I'm impressed."

"No guarantees," Jenn warned. "Soil composition can range widely over just a few feet, never mind over an entire huge ranch, and my soil databank is a work in progress at the moment."

"It's something, though." Gigi's eyes sparkled a little, as if she was starting to feel the *aha,* too.

As they shared a grin, footsteps sounded on the stairs.

Jenn spun toward the sound and Gigi started forward to cover her, but then relaxed, letting her hand fall from her weapon. "It's Matt." Raising her voice, she called, "A little warning next time, mister. We're a bit on edge down here in crime scene land."

"Sorry." He came through the archway, holding up his cell. "Guess my text didn't come through." His eyes went to Gigi first, softening and lingering there just long enough for Jenn's heart to give a bump of harmless envy. Then he glanced at her. "They got the driver."

"They…oh." If she hadn't already been sitting down, her legs might've folded. As it was, she went a little numb for a few seconds. "Dennison stepped in cow poop the last time he wore his boots."

Matt nodded as if that followed. "Good to know. You okay?"

"Yeah. I'm…" She stopped. Swallowed. "It wasn't the Investor, was it?" If it had been, he would've led with that info, after all. Besides, that hadn't been a crime lord's car; it'd had "lackey" written all over its unwaxed panels.

"Doesn't look like it."

"Who is it, then?"

"We're working on that right now. He's talking, but he's not saying much." Matt paused. "Nick is going to take over the questioning. He thought you might want to sit in on it upstairs, see if anything jogs your memory."

She buried the instinctive snarl that nothing seemed to be able to jog her memory, damn it. But who knew?

Maybe she would walk through the door into the viewing room on the other side of the one-way glass, take one look at the guy sitting opposite Nick, recognize her attacker and remember everything.

Maybe.

"Lead the way," she told Matt, rising to her feet and not letting herself wince at the twinges that reminded her that she'd already had a hell of a day.

Man up, she told herself. *This could be the break we need.*

As she followed them up the stairs, though, she wasn't thinking about the case or even the attacks. Instead, she couldn't stop thinking about the way Matt had looked at Gigi when he'd first come into the lab, as if he hadn't been able to help himself. The love between them was palpable, true. And it was exactly the kind of thing she'd wanted, back when she'd been looking to pair off and do the family thing. That hadn't worked out, though, and her ideas of what she needed had changed.

For a long time now, she had been telling herself that she wanted to be alone, that she liked the freedom of going out or not, dating or not as she chose. And if she chose "not" more often than otherwise, she had told herself that was okay. But now, as she hit the first floor and turned toward the interrogation rooms, she knew she had been wrong. Or maybe the too-familiar answer had been the right one at one point but wasn't anymore…because she was starting to realize that she didn't want to be on her own anymore.

No, she wanted a man who would look at her like Matt looked at Gigi. And mean it.

Chapter Six

As luck would have it—or maybe fate, irony, whatever—Nick was interviewing the driver in Interrogation Three, where he'd waited for Jenn that day six weeks earlier and handed her that tired load of "it's not you, it's me."

Only he hadn't even really said that. He'd just said it was over. Except now he was saying he still wanted her.

That doesn't matter right now. Focus. Get your head in the game.

She paused outside the closed door with the big number three on it, then kept going one more door down, to the viewing room that opened up from Interrogation Three. Long and narrow, with little more than a couple of chairs and a low shelving unit that held some random office supplies and a stack of sales brochures for various law enforcement supply stores, the viewing room wasn't exactly built for comfort.

Then again, she wasn't there to hang out. She was there to jog her damned unjoggable memory.

"You want company?" Gigi said from the open doorway. Matt stood behind her, not touching her yet somehow managing to look possessive and protective, as if he would take a piece out of anybody who tried to hurt her.

Jenn knew he would do the same for her if the opportunity arose—they both would—but this wasn't one of those times. "No, thanks. I think I need to do this one on my own."

Nerves fluttered at the thought of failure, though. She had put too much hope on Maya's hypnosis, only to wind up with the same damn gap in her memory. It was smaller now, granted, but what she'd remembered wasn't enough. And as the door swung shut and she looked through the one-way glass at the man who sat facing her, she saw only a stranger, and was badly afraid that this wasn't going to help, either.

The room's lone occupant was in his late twenties, average height or a bit below, with a buzzed-close skull trim that went ragged over the ears, suggesting it was a DIY job. He sported a pierced eyebrow, an intricate tribal tattoo on one forearm, sharp features and a truculent scowl as he stared down at the cuffs shackling him to the bolted-down table.

He looked like a hundred other guys she'd seen the Bear Claw cops wrestle into the holding area over the past few months, and like a thousand other guys she might walk past on the street without thinking twice about them. There wasn't any glimmer of recognition, no belly-twitch of instinct telling her that this was the guy. No nothing, really, except the dull throb of a headache setting up residence behind her eyeballs, and a growing frustration that made her want to crack her skull open and shake out the memories, like she was a cartoon character with tweeting birds circling her head.

She was getting punchy, she realized belatedly. But at the same time, she figured she had an excuse, given that she'd started the day up in the mountains and in less than ten hours had been hypnotized, nearly run over and kissed to within an inch of her life. And now she was standing in the room next to Interrogation Three, staring at the guy who had tried to kill her.

Allegedly, granted. But he'd been headed out of town in a hatchback that had matched Nick's description, with mismatched plates that later turned out to have been stolen. And when the cops had tried to pull him over, he'd bolted, leading them on a chase that had ended thanks to a tack strip laid down by a couple of rangers at the outskirts of the state park. The most preliminary of examinations on-scene had shown that the car had scrapes along one side and paint transfer that appeared to match Maya's SUV.

The analysts would confirm it with evidence and lab tests, but already there was no doubt in Jenn's mind: this was the guy who had tried to kill her.

Unfortunately, that didn't make him any less of a stranger to her.

She was just heaving a big sigh of disappointment when the door to the next room swung open and Nick strode into Interrogation Three.

Heat jolted through her at the sight of him—big, strong and intense, with a fierce expression that said he wasn't going to put up with any garbage from the suspect. His dark hair was slicked back in a stubby ponytail that made him look subtly dangerous, and he'd shed his heavy jacket to reveal the broad shoulders and muscled arms beneath his dark green sweater.

He slapped a file folder on the table, and said, "Okay. Let's get this over with."

His voice had a rough growl that fired Jenn's blood even further, reminding her of how he'd sounded right after they'd made love. But even as her heart thudded at the memory, he glanced up at the one-way glass... and looked nothing like the man who'd made love to her. Hell, he didn't even look like the guy who had met her and Maya out in the parking lot and announced he was going to stand in as their guard.

No, the man on the other side of the glass was cold and hard, with a faintly derisive edge to his tight-lipped smile.

A sinking shiver took root in her belly.

That was definitely Nick in there—it was his body, his face, his presence—but it wasn't the man she knew. This Nick had an aggressive jut to his jaw and moved with an unfamiliar swagger. And when he flipped open the file and gave it a quick once-over, his eyes held none of the alert intelligence she was used to. Instead, he was cold and chill, with a demeanor that practically screamed, *Go ahead and impress me. It won't be easy.*

The shiver grew as she recognized his 'tude from one of the other interrogation tapes she had watched. But the video hadn't really shown how his eyes went shark-dead, and it hadn't caught the menacing inflection in a voice gone cold as he said, "My colleagues tell me that you're not interested in cooperating with our investigation, Benjamin."

The suspect's eyes slid away from his. "Slider."

"What's that?"

"The name's Slider."

A sudden surge of nausea forced Jenn to breathe deeply a few times while the room around her threatened to spin. Benjamin. Slider. It didn't matter what he called himself—the man on the other side of the glass had tried to murder her. He'd planned to hit her with his car, running her over, crushing her to a pulp and—

A whimper bled from her lips. She might do her damnedest to be competent and self-sufficient in her everyday life—she had worked hard to get to that point—but she wasn't feeling at all tough and independent right now. In fact, she badly wanted to bury her face in a warm, solid chest, close her eyes and pretend this was all some strange nightmare.

There wasn't anybody there to lean on, though. She had sent Matt and Gigi away, and there was no way she was going back out there and admitting she needed moral support. So she breathed through her nose and made herself watch the interrogation unfolding in the next room.

"Well, then, Slider. Here's the deal…" Nick flipped open the folder and read silently, then shook his head and shut it once more. "We've got you and we've got the car. There's no question that you're going to go down for trying to run over my analyst earlier today. Question is, how far down are you going to go? You haven't lawyered up, which makes me think you might want to deal. So let's deal. Who are you working for?"

Slider just smirked a little and looked past him. "Nobody, man. My foot slipped on the gas, that's all."

Nick leaned in, eyes going hard and dark. "I get that your boss is a scary dude. But what you don't get is that I can be far scarier. And you don't want to get on my bad side."

He said it with enough venom that the suspect looked at him sidelong. "Oh, yeah?" Slider said, going for a sneer. But there was a thread of worry in it.

"Yeah. So let's talk."

If Jenn could have taken herself out of the equation, she thought she would've been fascinated watching Nick's technique.

It wasn't so much what he was saying as the way he was saying it, and his body language. He wasn't the nice-guy cop she'd seen interviewing the elderly grandma, the confident teammate who came to the task force meetings, or the wild-eyed rescuer who had hauled her up onto the roof of Maya's SUV. If anything, he was exactly the sort of guy someone like Slider would be a little afraid of.

She shivered with a sudden chill, and wished she'd brought her bomber. There was a thermostat near the door, but she didn't crank the heat. She stayed frozen, transfixed by the sight of a Nick she'd never seen before, at least not in person. He hadn't just morphed into a tough, no-nonsense interrogator; he'd turned into someone very much like the man sitting opposite him.

This wasn't the Nick she'd kissed a few hours ago, and it sure as hell wasn't the one she'd slept with two months ago. Yet somehow this was part of him, too.

Did she even know him at all? Had she ever?

Damn it, focus. But she suddenly didn't want to focus on Nick's interrogation, didn't want to be there. She wanted to be down in the lab, safe and dark, with layers of cement and guarded stairways between her and danger. And if that made her a fraud for pretending to be all brave and independent when she was really a coward deep down inside, she decided she could live with that, especially after a day like today.

Her legs barely supported her as she rose and turned for the door. But as she twisted the knob, Slider suddenly said, "You swear? You'll protect me, keep me out of jail?" His voice was different, almost earnest.

Surprise kicked through her, alongside hope. "Hot damn," she said softly, turning back. "He did it."

The glint in Nick's dark eyes said he knew it, too. He glanced up at the window, and it seemed for a second that their gazes met.

That was her imagination, of course. The glass was one-way.

Still, she moved back to the window and pressed her palm to the cool surface. "Keep going," she urged. "You're almost there."

Suddenly, it didn't matter that he had taken on a strange and intimidating persona, didn't even really matter that they'd complicated things between them with the kiss. All that mattered was that he was on the verge of getting something out of the man who had tried to murder her.

"Do it," she whispered as Nick moved in for the kill. "Break him."

"MAKE IT OFFICIAL, MAN," Slider urged Nick. The little punk was pale and sweating, not because he was detoxing or jonesing, but because he was truly scared, torn between his boss and the cops. "I want paperwork, something that says that if I tell you everything I know, you'll keep me out of jail and protect me from him."

Careful, Nick warned himself. *Keep it legal.* He'd be damned if the Investor walked because he'd screwed up protocol and left the lawyers some wiggle room. "I told you, I can't do that right here and now. But you have my word that I'll do my best on both of those things… assuming that what you give me is worth the trouble."

"Paperwork, man." But Slider's eyes were moving fast, going from the door to the one-way glass and back again. "I want assurances."

Nick didn't let himself look over at the window again. Didn't let himself wonder if Jenn was watching, if she'd recognized the bastard who'd tried to turn her into roadkill.

The dull, thudding anger he'd banked to make it through the interrogation threatened to spark at the reminder, and he leaned in, looming over Slider and getting a spurt of satisfaction when he shrank down a little in his chair. "You tried to kill a member of the Bear Claw police force. Do you really think you're going to get a better offer?"

"I want…" Slider hesitated, and for a second Nick thought he'd lost him, that the bastard was going to lawyer up. But then he said plaintively, "I want a deal, man."

"Then give me something to take to my bosses. Tell me who you work for."

It shouldn't have been possible for Slider to go even more sickly pale than he had been, but he managed it. "You know who I work for." It was little more than a whisper.

"Say his name."

"The Investor."

"Say his real name," Nick pressed, trying not to let the thin thread of excitement show in his eyes or voice. *Say it, you little creep. Give him to me.*

Could it finally be happening? Could they be getting the break they needed?

"That's all I know."

Damn it. "What does he look like?"

"I never saw him."

"How did you contact him?"

"Disposable cell." Slider looked mutinous. "Come on, man. Paperwork."

Nick scowled. "You haven't given me anything worth a fortune-cookie fortune, never mind any sort of deal. Keep trying." He thought he saw movement behind the one-way glass, though it was probably the power of suggestion. Still, though, it helped to think she was there. In an odd way, as much as it distracted him, it also made him stay centered, stay focused.

He'd always played best to an audience, after all.

"Okay, how about this?" he said, realizing he was going to have to change things up. "How about you tell me what's going to happen when he finds the stash?"

It was part bluff, part educated guess, but the surprise that flashed in Slider's eyes signaled a direct hit. "He'll leave the city, go somewhere else. He said he'd take me with him."

"What about the others?"

"There aren't any others, except for the paid informants. I was the last one he had working directly for him."

And despite what the Investor had promised, Slider suspected he wouldn't have survived the gig much longer, Nick surmised, both from the greasy flop sweats and the way the other man's words were coming easier now, starting to speed up and run over each other, as if he was afraid if he didn't keep talking, he'd wind up back out on the street, with only a matter of time before the Investor caught on that he'd been in custody. "That's it?" he pressed. "He's just going to leave with the rest of the drugs?"

Slider scoffed. "The drugs aren't half of it. Timms didn't just steal the stash—he got the virus and the programs, too. Everything that the boss needs to start up again in another city."

Nick didn't let the flush of victory show, but he mentally high-fived himself.

One of the main ingredients of the Death Stare drug came from trees that had been infected with a special bioengineered virus. The scientist who had developed it was dead, which meant that the Investor needed either the virus itself, or the complicated computer programs that could be used to make more of it. Except now it sounded as if he'd been double-crossed, the precious samples and programs stolen.

It fit. It played. And it explained why the bastard was still in town, why he was hunting down his former lieutenants and torturing them.

Apparently realizing—or at least hoping—that he'd scored, Slider straightened in his chair. "That's got to be good enough for a deal, right?"

Nick slouched a bit. "You still haven't told me anything I didn't know before." Which was a lie, and might skirt the line a little, but it would hold in court. "What else have you got? So far all you've told me is that the boss wants to find the stash and get out of Dodge. Yawn."

"Okay, how about this?" Slider's expression went calculating. "He's not going to leave without doing the brunette. Even if she never remembers his face, she's a loose end."

Nick's hands fisted before he could squelch the response, and he had to fight to keep his sudden fury from showing anywhere else. He didn't let himself glance at the window, didn't want her to see his rage. But whether he was proud of it or not, he was excited, too.

Slider had just confirmed that Jenn had seen the Investor's face. If she could just remember it, they could blanket the city with his image and send it to every law enforcement agency that had an acronym. Someone somewhere had to know who the bastard actually was.

There was no guarantee that Jenn would ever remember, though, and pressuring her wasn't going to help. So he needed to play this for all it was worth.

"Yawn," he said again, rolling his eyes. "I'm still not convinced. Tell me about these informants." Unfortunately, the Bear Claw P.D. already suspected there were leaks, both in the department itself and in the mayor's office. That was why the task force had been put together, and why its members were both trusted and tight-lipped.

Slider was done, though. He crossed his arms and leaned back. "Paperwork," he said. "Or I use the *L* word." And he wasn't talking about "love."

Knowing Tucker would kick his butt if their newest informant lawyered up now, Nick nodded. "Okay. I'll see what I can do." He shot the shackled punk an evil grin. "Don't go anywhere."

Slider told him to go do something anatomically impossible, and added a few curses that made up in volume for what they lacked in originality. Nick didn't care, though; he'd gotten what he wanted.

He kept up the bad-cop scowl as he came out of the room, then let it go as he shut the door at his back. He filled his lungs and then blew out all the air, long and slow, trying to flush as much of the old oxygen out of his system as he possibly could.

And with it, he exhaled the guy he'd been in that room.

He felt the meanness leave him, the chill cruelty and the desire to push and keep pushing, even if it hurt the person opposite him, even if it endangered them, because he couldn't let anything else matter but the case. The layers of Bad Cop flowed away from him, easing the too-tight muscles of his forehead, neck and shoulders, and making it easier for him to breathe.

He didn't mind Bad Cop any more than he did the other roles he slipped into and out of as easily as…well, as easily as breathing. Today, though, it had been an effort, not to be bad, but to keep the anger from tipping him over into something that went from bad to worse, and could have jeopardized the case rather than help crack it.

It was okay now, though. He had done it, and he thought they might have something to work with, and maybe even more to come after they rounded up Slider's beloved paperwork. The Investor's lackey was no saint—far from it—but he could prove very useful as an informant.

And if Nick kept reminding himself of that, maybe he'd stop wanting to bury his fist in the bastard's face, over and over again.

Maybe.

"Okay," he said on a final exhalation. "Okay." Feeling far more like himself, he opened his eyes. And found Jenn standing three paces away, staring at him. "Hey," he said, caught off guard, though he probably shouldn't have been. "Did you recognize him?"

"No. He wasn't the guy who attacked me in Dennison's apartment." But there was something going on behind her chocolate-brown eyes.

He pushed away from the wall to face her, instincts tingling. "You saw something, though. What was it?"

She hesitated then said, "Who was that in there?"

"Benjamin—"

"Not him. You. What happened in there? You weren't yourself...or were you?"

"Oh." Oh, hell. His stomach clutched as he realized he had scared her with the whole Bad Cop thing, probably made her question the guy he'd been when he was with her. He knew it would be better for both of them if she kept her distance, but he hadn't meant to terrify her.

It was inevitable, though, he supposed. In his experience, women—even the ones who said they understood his work, could handle it—couldn't face the reality of the guy he became undercover. Closed, distant and not like anything they wanted to be around.

She must have seen something in his eyes, but she didn't back off. Instead, she touched his sleeve. "Nick, talk to me. Please. I'm trying to understand what's going on here."

Knowing she was talking about more than just the interrogation, he glanced around and took a couple of steps away from her, aiming for the next door over, where the unlit bulb over the door indicated that Interrogation Two was unoccupied. "Let's take this out of the hallway."

"No." She backed up, and at the flash of hurt in her eyes, he remembered too late what had happened the last time he'd gotten her into an interrogation room. "Here and now. I want an explanation."

Or what? the hard, closed-off part of him wanted to demand. He didn't owe her anything. More, it would be better—easier, at least on a personal level—if she walked away. Yes, he still wanted her, wanted her with a burning ache that rode low in his gut and pressed beneath his heart, but nothing had changed, really. That was the thing, though—he'd never really explained why he'd pushed her away. And even the hard part of him knew that had been a jerkwad move.

She deserved better. Always had.

Hell, he should tell her the truth. Not that he had lied, really, but he hadn't told her everything. He hadn't thought it was necessary, hadn't known at the time that he would have so much damn trouble letting go.

He'd been silent too long, because she grimaced and shook her head. "Never mind. I thought… Well, I guess I thought wrong." She turned to leave, and he told himself to let her go.

He followed and caught her arm instead. "No. You weren't wrong. You were very right—I owe you an explanation. But I need you to wait here for a minute." When her eyes narrowed, he added softly, "Please, Jenn."

After a brief hesitation that felt far longer than it probably was, she nodded. "Okay."

It didn't take him long to brief Tucker on the interrogation and get the ball rolling on Slider's deal. Then he grabbed his bomber, caught her arm once more and urged her down the hallway. "Come on."

She let him lead her away from the interrogation rooms to the stairwell leading up. "Where are we going?"

"You'll see."

Chapter Seven

He took her to the roof of the P.D. headquarters, where they found the air crisp and chill, the sky leaden with an incoming early-winter storm. The building wasn't the tallest in the city, but there was enough of a vantage that Bear Claw City spread out around them, looking like a half-size diorama, and far more peaceful from up above than it was down on the street level.

Jenn hadn't ever brought Nick up here, didn't know how he'd figured out it was one of her favorite escapes when she needed a five-minute break from the basement. Or maybe he didn't know. Maybe he'd found it on his own, and liked it for the freedom and wide-open spaces.

Darn him.

It was hard for her to stay mad up here, though. Not when the city—her city—was spread out around her, reminding her that she had a ton to be grateful for. She had a great job in a city she loved. And she was still alive, thanks to Nick.

She drew a deep breath, filling her lungs with air that shouldn't have smelled of the distant mountains, but somehow did. She loved the way the edges of the city sprawl petered out to the patchwork blocks of snow-shrouded ranchland in some places, and bumped up against the stark green and rocky open stretches of the state forest in others. The nearest mountains were threaded with brilliant white veins of snow, laced with ski lifts and studded with lodges. All of it felt very vibrant to her, very alive, even from a distance.

Still, though, she was all too conscious of Nick standing a few paces away, watching her with guarded eyes and a lingering edge of the toughness that he'd shown in the interrogation room. The wind tugged his hair out of its stubby ponytail, making him look untamed.

Her too-sharp awareness of him brought a shiver that was quickly amplified by a gust that cut right through her sweater and thermal layer. She crossed her arms and hugged herself for warmth, glancing over at him and doing her damnedest not to let her thoughts show on her face. "Okay, we're out here. Talk fast. It's too cold."

"Here." Nick shrugged out of his bomber and draped it around her shoulders, snapping it closed at her throat to form a warm, heavy cape. The fleece-lined leather surrounded her instantly with body heat and a heady, masculine scent that tugged against bittersweet memories.

"You'll freeze," she said, though the protest sounded halfhearted, even to her.

"I'll be fine." He shoved his hands in his pockets and blew out a breath that made white ghosts in the air. Somehow he didn't look any smaller without the heavy coat. If anything, the dark green sweater made him look bigger and broader through the chest.

He's just being a good guy, she told herself. *Don't read too much into it.* Especially not when this good-guy mode carried more than a bit of the bad-boy edge in the hard lines of his jaw and the steady steel in his eyes. "So?" she said finally. "Tell me about the guy I saw in Interrogation Three."

"That's me," he said, meeting her eyes. "But this is me, too. I'm the guy who lived with you for two of the best weeks of my life, the guy who broke it off with you and didn't explain why, the guy who kissed you earlier and then ducked talking about it…and I'm also a guy who can worm his way into the tightest organization by talking the right smack and doing whatever it takes to make himself be what the bosses need." He paused. "I've been a mule, an enforcer, even a killer. I'm all of those guys, Jenn, and that's the problem."

She shivered involuntarily, but wouldn't—couldn't—let that drive her away. "What problem, exactly?" she asked, though she could start to guess, had already gotten part of the way there just by watching him and realizing she couldn't trust what she was seeing.

"It's not something you can understand until you've been there."

You have no idea where I've been, she wanted to snap. She didn't, though, because that wasn't his fault. When they'd been together, it had been about the fun, the excitement, the sex. They hadn't really gone out, hadn't really talked about their pasts—it had all been in the moment, most of it in the bedroom. That had been their agreement, after all, and there hadn't been any reason to take it deeper.

Now, maybe, there was.

So she kept her voice and her eyes level, didn't let him see the nerves that flared when she said, "Try me." And, yes, those were nerves. Because if they were sharing, at some point it was going to have to go both ways, and he wasn't the only one with monsters in his closet.

He hesitated, then said, "I have an ex-wife and two sons who I only see a few times a year."

"You…oh." She actually took a step back, away from him. Not because he looked particularly fierce just then—although he did—but because where she might've been braced to learn about some of the awful things he'd needed to do undercover, she suddenly found that she wasn't braced for this.

She didn't have any right to feel a spark of anger, maybe even jealousy, at learning he had an ex. They were grown-ups, were bound to have pasts. But coming from a tight, loving family like she did, there was an instinctive flinch at the thought of him staying away from his kids. She wasn't an idiot; she knew it happened, was more the norm than the exception in some places. It just seemed late for her to be hearing this now. Especially given that she had told him almost from the beginning that she was a widow, and that things hadn't been good between her and Terry.

She hadn't told him how bad, though, or what form the fallout had taken.

"Stacia and I got along great at the beginning," he said, so softly that Jenn might've thought he was thinking out loud, except that he was looking right at her. "I was just out of the academy when we met, bumping up from rookie when we got married, working at a local P.D. in southern Florida."

"Was that where you grew up?"

"She did, not me. I moved there after college, because I was looking for something that wasn't anything like New York. Pensacola wasn't the city and it wasn't freezing four months out of the year. As far as I was concerned, it was heaven." He shrugged. "And it was, for a while. But two kids later, with me working for the DEA, things started falling apart."

"Once you started working undercover," Jenn said, beginning to get past the sting enough to see the pattern.

She'd heard it before. Heck, she'd seen it more times than she cared to remember, mostly among SWAT members, like Terry had been. Those of his buddies who'd been married rarely stayed that way, thanks to the crazy hours, the mental and physical realities of the work, and the distance it created.

For a long time, it had seemed that she and Terry were the only ones who knew how to make it work, knew how to keep the flame going through the ups and downs of SWAT work. Then everything had hit the fan, and she'd learned how wrong she had been. How badly he had played her, fooled her.

"Yeah," Nick said, and for a second she thought he was agreeing that she had been an idiot to believe her husband's lies. A split second later, though, she realized he was talking about undercover work and how it had wrecked his own marriage. "I turned into That Guy," he continued. "You know, the one who gets weird and distant when the work gets ugly. I thought I was doing the right thing by not telling Stacia what I was going through, what I was up against, because I didn't want her worrying all the time." He grimaced. "Anyway, you know cops, which means you can probably fill in the rest. The better I got at my job, the more they put me undercover, which meant time away from home. And when I was home, I was That Guy. A stranger, Stacia said. I tried like hell to be the man she remembered, the one she fell in love with, but it wasn't enough."

"And the kids?" She couldn't imagine it was somehow better for them to only see him a few times a year.

"Nicholas and Turner." His expression twisted. "I'd show you pictures, but I don't carry anything that can link me to them, or the rest of my family. Just in case."

"I…" She trailed off, realizing suddenly that maybe he was right. Maybe she didn't really get what his life was like. She had only really seen him as another cop— he was something of a rock star among the detectives, yes, and she had liked that about him. She'd known he was more than that, just as SWAT cops were more than the norm. But maybe she hadn't thought about what it really meant to do what Nick did, day in and day out.

What would it be like, not being able to carry her parents' pictures with her, or even have their numbers in her cell? She tightened his bomber around her, suddenly far colder than even the wind.

Was that how he lived back in Florida? As a solo operator, only managing to be a part of his family during carefully timed gaps in his schedule?

"Stacia remarried a year after the divorce was finalized," he said, the words seeming to come easier now for him, even though they were getting harder and harder for her to hear. "Paul is a great guy, and a way better father than I was. He adopted the boys, took them as his own, and I…well, I'm more of an uncle to them, like I am with my brother's and sister's kids. The cool uncle who shows up a few times a year with good presents." His words were far more matter-of-fact than the bleakness at the back of his eyes.

Or maybe she just wanted to see that, wanted to think he had regrets.

"Why didn't you quit?" She hadn't meant to say it, and shook her head. "Never mind. Not my business."

"It's okay." He shrugged and looked out toward the ski slopes, which were growing fuzzy with a band of incoming snow. "At the time, I thought I was indispensable, that if I didn't take the assignments nobody would. Or even if they did, they couldn't possibly get the jobs done as fast and with as little collateral damage as I was managing." He glanced back at her. "This was when the drug traffic was at its absolute worst in Miami. We were fighting a rearguard action, with new organizations cropping up as fast as we could take them down. Faster, even. So, no. I couldn't make myself quit, not even to save my marriage." He grimaced. "Partly because I knew damn well she was right, that she and the boys were better off without me. At least then they didn't have to wonder whether I was coming home."

Pain tugged somewhere deep inside her. "What about now?"

"Miami still has its dark side, but it's not as bad as it was."

"So why not quit now and try the family thing again?"

His grin was rueful and very self-aware. "Because deep down inside, I still think I'm indispensable, and I still can't see myself giving it up. Besides, I'm good at being the cool uncle."

In other words, he didn't want a family more than he wanted the job. She shouldn't blame him for that— heck, she had moved three states on forty-eight hours' notice, just for a chance to get back in a crime lab for half the money she had been making.

Still, though, it hurt to say, "So that's it? That's all you want for yourself?"

"It's about what's fair, and what I can offer to someone else…which isn't much." He turned away from the mountains and crossed to her, so his big body was blocking out the wind and he was very close to her, looking down into her eyes as he said, "Since Stacia and I broke up, I've only dated very casually, had the occasional no-strings affair, a week, two at the most. Nothing that ran the risk of hurting anybody. Until you."

Her blood heated, though with anger rather than desire. Or maybe both. It was hard to tell sometimes with him. "Is that why you dumped me? Because you thought I was starting to pick out china or something? That's a hell of a leap."

Maybe she'd been thinking in terms of extending their relationship, taking it up a notch, but she hadn't said anything to him. More, that was hardly the same thing as expecting forever and a family, complete with a puppy and a picket fence.

The thought of it tugged at her far more than she would've expected, though. Far more than she was comfortable with.

He tipped his hand in a "sort of" gesture. "It wasn't you, it was me."

"Ha. Original."

"I mean it, though." He took her hand. He didn't lift it to his heart as he might have before, letting her feel how hard it was beating, how much she turned him on. Instead, he looked down at their joined hands. "What we had was great, Jenn. Better than great. It was amazing, wonderful, crazy…and it was the crazy part that had me worried. When I found out the agency wanted me to stay here in Bear Claw until the Death Stare case wraps up, it was like Christmas came early. I wanted to tell you right away, even picked up my phone to call you…but then I saw how I'd programmed your number into my cell just as 'J.P.' Nothing else. And even that would be something I'd erase the second the case was over. Which reminded me why I didn't get to be in a real relationship."

Ignoring how her throat tightened at knowing that he had been excited, too, she said, "We said it was nothing serious, just two adults having fun."

"Two adults who were living together, damn near inseparable?" He met her eyes. "Tell me you weren't counting the days, the hours, dreading when the weekend came and I got on that plane."

She didn't deny it. Couldn't. "And I suppose you were looking forward to it, figuring it was the easy way to end things, clean and simple, no hurt feelings?"

"No, damn it. That's the point." He squeezed her fingers. "I was crazy about you, Jenn. I wanted to stay and be with you, more than almost anything."

Almost. That, apparently, was the key word with him, especially when he was weighing the value of having a life against doing his job. In a way it was admirable. Mostly, though, it was irritating. Heartbreaking.

"You were crazy about me," she said, "past tense. Meaning you're not anymore. But earlier you said you still want me. Pick one, Nick. Either you want to be with me or you don't."

He brushed his knuckles across her cheek, though she wasn't crying, wouldn't let herself show that weak-

ness. Not now, with him. Still, though, it brought a pang
when he said, "I shouldn't want you if I know I can't
have you."

You could have, though. You did. She shook her head,
torn between anger and a hollow, echoing sadness. "You
can just shut off your emotions like that?"

"No, but I can do my best to override them if I know
it's the better course of action."

And that was the thing, she realized as her anger
drained, leaving the hollowness behind. He was really
trying to do the right thing, at least as he saw it. She
might not agree with his methods, or even his conclu-
sions, but she could admit he hadn't been trying to be
a jerk.

In his own way, he had already known what had
solidified for her today: the things that made him one
of the DEA's best undercover agents—his ability to
play many roles, be many men and, more, the need that
drove him to do the job—made him a bad bet for a relationship. It wasn't learning of his divorce that made
her think that, either; it had been seeing him in the interrogation room, and then after, when she'd watched
him shed the role of Bad Cop and put his detective face
back on.

It had been eerie. Unsettling. And it had warned her
of what she already understood, deep down inside—
that she didn't know him, not really.

Aware of the warm pressure of his fingers, the steadi-
ness of him waiting out there in the cold for her reaction,
she sighed. "You could have told me the truth, Nick."

Something sparked in his eyes, but he nodded.
"You're probably right. Hell, you *are* right. I just didn't

figure that out until way too late." He paused. "If it helps any, this is the first time I've been in this situation."

"Breaking up with someone you're still going to see every day?"

"Ending it with someone I still want to be with."

Her breath whistled out. "Don't," she said softly. "Don't say things like that, and don't kiss me again. Not unless you're willing to do something about it."

It wasn't quite an ultimatum, but it was close. What else could she do, though? Now that she knew what was really going on with him, she wouldn't be able to hang on to the low-grade anger that had been keeping her sane when she saw him. And even knowing that she wasn't seeing all of him, she was still desperately attracted to the guy standing in front of her. If he kissed her, kept kissing her…well, she would be in serious danger of making a big mistake.

A deliciously fun mistake. Probably one of the best mistakes of her life. But a mistake nonetheless.

He didn't say anything for a moment, and her heart momentarily bumped at the thought that he was going to tell her that he'd changed his mind, that they should go back to the way things had been between them, no strings, just a blazing affair, with the deeper things left unsaid.

Even knowing that wouldn't be enough for her, and that she would just be setting herself up for heartbreak by getting involved with him, her pulse quickened. Because when she came down to it, the sex had been fantastic. Good enough to overrule her common sense, and then some.

But then he nodded. "You're right. I won't…well, I won't. That's a promise." He paused. "And I know it's probably too little, too late, but I want you to know that I'm sorry. Not for getting involved with you—I wouldn't trade those twelve days for anything. But I wish like hell I had ended it differently. I wish I had told you all this back then, and asked you to understand."

"That would've been better." Would it really, though? Would it have been any easier for her to know he still wanted her all that time, only not enough to take the risk of being with her?

"I'm sorry. Forgive me?"

Knowing there was no way to go back and have a do-over, she forced a smile. "Well, seeing as you've now saved my life twice, I guess I owe you one."

His expression went fierce. "You don't owe me a damn thing."

"Still. I forgive you. I even understand, sort of." Because the more she thought of it, the more she really remembered how it had been between them, she had to admit that "crazy" had been the exact right word for it. And if back then he had told her the things he'd just revealed, she would have wanted them to stay involved, would've forced herself to let it be enough. And despite all the warnings, she would've been utterly shattered when he left.

She had been crazy about him. Still was, really. Now, though, she saw the pitfalls.

"You're sure?"

After giving his hand one last squeeze, she let go and eased away from him. "I'm sure. I'm—" The door leading to the roof swung open, and sent a jolt of adrenaline through her.

Nick put himself in front of her and drew his sidearm in a single deadly move, then let out a low curse as a man stepped through. "Damn it, Tucker. A little warning would be nice. We're a bit twitchy here."

"I trust your twitches," the other man said. He stood in the doorway, propping the heavy door with his shoulder. "Which is why I came up here to talk to you both unofficially rather than doing it in front of the others."

"Doing what?" Jenn asked, her stomach sinking when all she could think about was her probationary period, her job. *Please don't fire me; I'm trying my hardest. I didn't mean to lose the evidence.*

"Assigning you with an official guard, twenty-four/seven, until the Investor is off the streets."

"An official…oh." She stopped, nonplussed, trying to catch up when her brain had gone in a totally different—and admittedly paranoid—direction.

This wasn't about her job, at least not directly. It was about the case…and the fact that Slider had said the Investor wouldn't leave town until she was no longer a threat. A loose end. Which she had so far filed under "things I don't want to think about." She was thinking about it now, though, and suddenly realizing that she wasn't going to be truly safe anywhere. Not in the lab and not in her home…and she'd be damned if she ran back to the mountain safe house when she had work to do.

She was in serious danger, though. That was probably why Nick had brought her up to the roof rather than down the street to a coffee shop or something. He'd wanted her on P.D. property, and had figured there was a low risk of the Investor seeing her and getting a sniper into place in the short amount of time they had been visible, vulnerable.

A sick shudder ran through her at the idea, and the

realization that was how she was going to have to think for the foreseeable future.

"I'll do it," Nick said.

He had hesitated, though. More, she felt the sudden tension in the air between them, the quiver that said he wasn't sure this was a good idea.

"Jenn?" Tucker said. "Does that work for you? If not, I can assign—"

"It's fine." She nodded, taking a deep breath to settle the sudden queasiness in the pit of her stomach. "Better than fine. If I have to deal with a guard, I'd rather it be Nick than—" *Anyone else,* she started to say, but bit off the words, not wanting to give Tucker—or Nick—the wrong idea. So she swallowed and said again, "It's fine. He can have the couch."

Tucker cleared his throat at that one, suggesting it was TMI, but she didn't care. The air was clear between her and Nick now, and she didn't intend to play any games. Hadn't ever intended to. He was the chameleon, not her.

And he'd hesitated before saying he would guard her. That shouldn't have stung. Because it did, her chin came up. "What about using me to draw out the Investor?"

"No way," Nick said sharply, rounding on her. "You're not playing bait."

She ignored him and said to Tucker, "Tell me you're considering it."

"It's been discussed."

Nick transferred his glare. "Why wasn't I part of this conversation?"

Tucker ignored that and said to Jenn, "We're not ready to make the move right now, but it's on the table."

She nodded, heart thudding against her ribs. "I'll

do it. Whenever, wherever you say. Whatever it takes to get this guy."

"For now, just keep yourself safe and see if you can remember his face."

"Yes, sir."

"Now that we've got that settled, consider me on guard duty as of now," Nick said, scowling as he holstered his sidearm, leaving the snap undone. "I'll cover her whenever she's out of the lab, but if you keep the uniforms on the access points, I can keep working my angles when she's safe underground." He wasn't looking at her, his anger palpable.

"Hello?" she said, irritation sparking to match his. "I'm right here."

"Sorry," he grated. Then he stopped himself and blew out a long, slow breath, just like he had done outside the interrogation room. Meeting her eyes, he said, "I'm sorry, really. I just wasn't prepared for the bait thing. I should've been, I know."

"If you were in my shoes, you would've volunteered two weeks ago."

"You're right. But that doesn't make this any easier for me."

"It's not about you."

His eyes went shadowed, but he didn't argue. Instead, he said, "Like I said, I'll stick close to you whenever you're out of the lab, so you need to promise me—and Tucker and the other analysts—that you won't leave the lab without letting me know. If I'm not there for some reason and you absolutely can't put off whatever you need to do, then you'll check in with Tucker or one of the other ranking detectives, and they'll hook you up with an escort."

"What about crime scenes?"

It was Tucker who shook his head. "You're going to be strictly in the lab until further notice."

She hoped none of the others had blabbed her hatred of crime scenes, that this was simply protocol, or him being safe. "With all due respect, I'd rather not—" She stopped herself, though, blew out a breath, and said, "Yes, sir."

There was no point in insisting on something that would make more work for cops who had far more important things to do. Like find the man who was trying to kill her.

Right now, though, she was just as happy that Tucker had vetoed using her as bait. She had needed to make the offer—and had meant it, still did—but the thought of actually doing it had cold sweat greasing her skin beneath the heavy bomber she still had clutched around her.

Where before it had made her feel as if Nick was surrounding her, protecting her, now it seemed like a thin shield between her and the outside world, and the man who hunted her. Nick would still be protecting her, it was true, but their conversation had put a new distance between them, a new level of understanding.

He wanted her, but only on his terms.

Tucker and Nick talked for another minute, going over logistics, but in the end it was decided that they would stick with the basic plan Nick had outlined. He would escort her home, stay with her overnight and then bring her back to the lab in the morning. In addition, there would be two surveillance teams, one following her, the other keeping watch on the apartment building and its interior camera feeds.

They might not think twice about a well-dressed businessman going into her building, Jenn thought with a tug of nerves, but they would definitely notice if he went for her door, and they would sound the alarm.

She was trying to be okay with all the surveillance, trying to tell herself that it was part of the case, another way they might catch the Investor. It was easier to think of it like that than really admitting, even to herself, that she was going to be practically on house arrest because a madman wanted her dead.

"Okay, we've got a plan," Tucker said, and headed for the stairs. "I'll let the others know, and see if the D.A. has come through yet with that paperwork on your informant."

Nick gestured for Jenn to precede him down the stairs, but as she passed, he caught her hand. "Hang on a sec. We got interrupted there, but I wanted to say it again—I'm sorry I broke things off like that. I should've told you everything right from the beginning. I just didn't realize that it—that you were going to turn out to be so important. And when I did…well, I didn't handle things well."

She nodded, not trusting herself to speak when he was that close to her, when he was touching her. Even though he'd made it clear that he could only offer her the same short-term fling they'd had before, only this time without the craziness or the secret hope that it would turn into something more, her blood still burned at the pressure of his grip on her arm, the nearness of his body beneath the athletic sweater and the fog of his breath on the air between them.

Bad idea, she told herself. *He's not your lover anymore. He's just your bodyguard.*

And that, too, was a hell of a thought.

Tugging her arm away, she said, "It's okay, Nick. It's over and done, and we're moving on…. But given that we're going to be up in each other's business for the time being, I've got a favor to ask."

"Anything." He said it as if he meant it, though they both knew it wasn't true.

"I don't like seeing you be all these different people. It freaks me out. When we're together, especially at the apartment, I'd appreciate it if you didn't play any roles with me."

He hesitated a moment, then nodded. "Agreed. I'll be myself when we're alone." As she headed down the stairs, she thought she heard him murmur, "I always am, with you."

That had to be her imagination, though. Either that, or it was a lie. Because she had seen too many faces of Nick Lang to believe he was always being himself with her. In fact, she wondered if he even knew who he really was anymore.

Chapter Eight

Nick figured it would be weird going back to Jenn's apartment for the first time since he'd moved out. The sadness caught him by surprise, though, hitting him the moment he came through the door and caught himself starting to shrug out of his jacket and hang it on the curved coatrack.

Instead, he kept it on and pulled his piece.

"Close the door and wait here," he said quietly, and moved into the apartment, senses on high alert. The apartment was under full surveillance, but he still wasn't willing to trust that the bastard hadn't slipped through the perimeter.

As he crossed the living room, scanned the open-concept kitchen and headed for the two bedrooms and a bath that opened off the back, he had a hell of a time staying professional when just about every damn thing he touched or even saw triggered memories.

There was the couch they had spent countless hours on together, cuddling while watching the TV, or just talking; there were the pillows and blankets they had tossed on the floor one night, so they could have an impromptu picnic in front of the fake fire crackling from the flat screen; and the surviving lamp of a pair still sat next to the sofa, alone now because they had broken its mate when their lovemaking had spun them off the couch and they knocked over an end table.

And everywhere he looked, he saw puzzles. Huge, glossy two-dimensional puzzles with intricate designs and thousands of pieces hung on the walls, sealed and framed. Smaller 2D designs stood in boxy frames on the mantel and bookcase, while other flat surfaces held beautifully detailed three-dimensional puzzles—a ship in a bottle, the Eiffel Tower, the skeleton of a horse suspended in midgallop.

They weren't just puzzles Jenn had completed, either, though that was what he had assumed at first. He'd been blown away to learn that she'd designed and made them, then sold the plans to a boutique company she'd been working with for years.

She had told him—during a rare moment when a conversation over buffalo burgers and beer had gone deeper than their usual surface chats—that she had taken up the hobby when her husband had been working the late shift, giving her something to do that was hers. She hadn't told him that the projects reflected her mood, but he had guessed as much when he'd seen that she had gone from family scenes to bleak black-and-white photos of windswept mountains and empty skies, and from there, more recently, to pictures taken in and around Bear Claw.

Now, seeing a half-finished 3D prototype on the dining table, he tried not to wonder what it meant that she was working on a small, exquisitely detailed cottage with a cute yard and picket fence, but nobody home.

Body tight, he moved into the second bedroom, which she used as a home office. The texts, journals and forensic reference books should have reminded him of the case, but the desk and its swivel chair put him in mind of something very different, as did the bathroom, with its oversize tub and shower, and the fluffy blue towels he'd wrapped around her before carrying her to the bedroom when the hot water had run out.

Focus, damn it. There was no reason for him to be so distracted. Especially not after the talk they'd had back on the roof. He had cleared the air and apologized; she had accepted. End of story. He shouldn't be obsessing about the past at this point, and there was no reason that seeing the apartment again should hit him so hard.

Then again, maybe it made sense. By the time he'd moved out of the house he and Stacia had bought, their relationship had been over and done with, and when he'd visited after the fact, things had been different, moved around and changed, making him feel like a stranger, a visitor. Here, though, everything was the same…including his and Jenn's chemistry.

Gritting his teeth, he checked her bedroom, with its soothing blues and greens, and unexpected zebra-striped pillows, and too many memories to process.

With his pulse thudding in his temples, he let the surveillance team know that they were secure, and reconfirmed that they were monitoring the exterior and hallways only, with no interior bugs, infrared or amplifiers. He didn't care what they thought about his insistence; he just wanted to know that whatever got said between him and Jenn stayed private, tonight and for however long this took.

He didn't dare think about how long that might be. Part of him wished it were already over; part of him was hoping it took a long damn time. And he needed to get his head screwed on tight, or he was going to drive both of them nuts.

"All clear," he announced gruffly, waving Jenn in from the entryway. "Door locked?"

"Locked, bolted and security set." She tossed her coat on the rack, started to hold out a hand for his, hesitated and then held out her hand, anyway. "Let me take your coat. Feel free to crank the heat. I've got it on a timer, and we're home a little earlier than my usual."

Some of his tension leaked away as she hung up his coat and put her bag in the office. They had both brought their laptops home so they could work remotely; he dropped his bag near the couch, this time doing a better job of blocking the sensory memories that popped up at the sight of those pillows and throw blankets, and the empty space between the coffee table and the flat screen, where he'd made love to her for the last time.

Okay, so he wasn't doing that good a job of blocking the memories. He would manage it, though. She needed protection, and whether or not she wanted to hear it, he owed her. More, he wanted to be here, wanted more… but that was his problem, and he wasn't going to make it hers, too.

So he headed for the thermostat, bumped the temp a few degrees and said, "You want me to call in a delivery for dinner?"

She turned back. "Is it safe?"

"We can make it be."

After a brief hesitation, she nodded. "I'll get the menus."

It wasn't the first time they had gone through the local takeout options together, but the flinch factor was starting to mellow out, he found, as if his body was figuring out that they were back in the apartment, but things weren't going to be the same as they had been before.

Eventually, they settled on Asian fusion and put in the order, and he okayed it through the perimeter when it came. They broke open a bottle of wine—more for her than for him, as he was on duty and capped it at a half glass—ate at the breakfast bar and stuck to neutral topics—the weather, the case, Matt's early performance as the city's mayor and his old job as a SWAT team leader in her hometown.

"My dad had a ton of respect for him," she said with a soft, reminiscing smile before dipping into the pad Thai. "He was sorry when Matt left town."

"Your dad was a cop?" How had he not known that?

She nodded fondly. "He's retired now. My mom's retired, too—she was a genetics professor, still teaches sometimes at the university. I was a surprise for them, pretty late in life."

"And you combined their interests by going into forensics."

"Dad wanted me to be a cop. Mom wanted another scientist in the family. It seemed like a good match, not just for them, but for me, too."

"You're good."

"I love it. I missed it." She glanced over at him. "You never asked me what happened, why I left and why I'm on probation now. Did you pull the files?"

Before, when she had hinted at the subject of her husband and a scandal at her old crime lab, he had changed the subject, figuring they were together in the present, in the moment, and the past didn't matter.

Now, though, he said, "Nope. I figured it was your

call to tell me, or not." Then added, "Besides, it wasn't like we were doing baggage at ten paces. We were just going with the flow and keeping things simple."

"Until today." She slid him a sidelong look. "Do you want to hear it?"

Did he? The smarter part of him said there was no point to it, that he'd only told her about Stacia and the boys as part of explaining why he'd fumbled their breakup. Another part of him, though, said this would be easier if they were friendly. And, more, that if she was relaxed with him, felt safe with him, she might be more likely to regain those lost memories. So maybe it would be in the best interests of everyone—him, her, the case—for him to put her at ease.

But was that a role, a manipulation? He had promised to be himself with her, after all. And, damn it, he didn't know the answer to that one, because wasn't acting a fact of life? The moment somebody else came into the room—or on the phone, the video chat, whatever—the people involved were acting, juggling agendas, trying to get their end results.

The way he saw it, it wasn't so much about putting on a role, but about how much effort it took.

Heck, that was one of the things he'd liked about their time together—he hadn't had to think about his performance. It had just flowed, felt easy, felt right.

And this, too, felt right, though there was an edge of danger to the rightness, as if something inside him was warning that this wasn't smart, even though it seemed it should be.

Ignoring those warnings, he nodded. "Yeah. I'd like to hear about it, if you wouldn't mind telling me."

The look she shot him suggested he wasn't the only

one who wasn't sure this was a good idea, or why they were even doing it. They had agreed to move on, hadn't they? He didn't take it back, though. And after a moment, she nodded, pushed away the pad Thai, refilled her wineglass and said, "Okay. Here goes."

"You know that I'm a widow, that I was married to a SWAT cop," Jenn began. "Terrence Prynne. Terry. We met through my father, of course, and clicked right away. We kept things pretty casual at first, because I was still in school—he was six years older and already established on the force. Once I graduated, though, and got my job—he helped out there, though I didn't know it for sure at the time—we got more serious. He asked me to marry him on Thanksgiving, in front of my family." She paused. "At the time, I thought it was because he knew how important they were to me." Later she had realized he enjoyed playing to an audience. "We had a June wedding and a perfect marriage…at least it seemed that way to me."

It had been a long while since she'd thought about those days, and this was the first time since his death that she could remember thinking back without being furious. She was still angry, yes, but it had mellowed to disillusionment rather than ire. He was gone, after all. He couldn't apologize or make amends—which he probably wouldn't have done, anyway—and she couldn't tell him what she thought of him.

She just needed to let it go.

Realizing that made it easier for her to continue. "Looking back, I probably should have seen the signs— the way he could buy a boat, a fancy car and all the boy toys he ever wanted, and still had enough money for us to have a nice house in a nice neighborhood. We had separate accounts. I bought the groceries and staples, he handled the mortgage and utilities. At the time, I thought it seemed like a reasonable division of the finances. It wasn't until later, when I was on my own, that I found out I didn't have any real credit history of my own because he'd been paying the big bills. More, he was hiding money."

She stalled, wondering whether this was enough. Wondering whether it was too much. Wondering whether it was the wine talking, and if she would regret all this in the morning.

Nick nudged the pad Thai back toward her. "You should eat more. You've had a hell of a day."

She didn't know why she obeyed, or why taking a bite and pausing a moment to chew and swallow made it easier for her to speak. "We'd been married almost four years when it happened. We had been talking about starting a family, but I was hesitating. I'd like to say it was because something deep inside me knew things weren't right between us, but that would be a case of hindsight being twenty-twenty. The truth is, I loved my job and I wasn't sure I was ready to cut back on overtime and curtail things in order to be a mom."

It occurred to her then that maybe she was more like Nick than she'd wanted to admit, at least in that regard. She hadn't wanted Terry's baby enough to rearrange her life, especially knowing that she would be the one cutting back her hours, organizing the day care and being the full-time parent along with a full-time job. Meanwhile, he would keep going out on calls, keep leaving her up late at night, waiting for him to call or, worse, for one of his buddies to knock.

"I didn't want to be a single parent," she said softly, realizing for the first time that it had been as simple as that, and as complicated. "Anyway, things were fine when he left that morning. I kissed him at the door and headed to work, not having any hint that my life was about to blow up." It hadn't been a phone call or a knock on the door, after all. She had been in the lab, heard the hot call go out on the dispatch radio they kept turned low…and twenty minutes later, she'd heard the shout of "officer down"…and then Terry's name. "I knew things weren't ever going to be the same after that. I just didn't know how bad it was going to get."

She went for another bit of pad Thai, was surprised to find the carton empty.

"Here." Nick nudged his orange chicken in her direction.

"I'm not really hungry anymore." She took a nibble, though. "Losing him was the worst thing I'd ever been through, bar none. He left that morning with everything fine, and then…he wasn't there anymore." She had forgotten that part, she realized. Or it had become so much less important given what followed. "The last thing I said to him was about garbage day and recycling, because we'd missed the week before and I needed his help lugging a dead AC to the curb."

Little things. Normal things.

How had her life felt so real and solid when there had been so many lies going on underneath the surface? Anger kicked, as it always did, along with self-disgust.

"Anyway," she said. "It wasn't until a few weeks later, after the funeral, that the bad stuff started to come out." She had been back at work by then, enduring her coworkers' painful sympathy, her parents' helpless comfort.

"He was on the take," Nick said quietly. "Wasn't he?"

She cut him a sharp look. "I thought you said you didn't crack the files."

"Tucker mentioned it, asked if I wanted the story. I turned him down."

She nodded. Of course Tucker would've said something, especially once she and Nick got involved. No doubt the whole department knew some version of the story—she hadn't kept it hidden. She had only told her version of it to Matt, though. And now Nick. She didn't know why she was telling him, really. Just because he'd told her the truth about their breakup, that didn't make them friends.

"Terry had sold out," she confirmed, surprised that it still hurt a little to say. Not just because she'd fallen for his lies, but because he'd been a SWAT cop, a hero. And heroes weren't supposed to do things like that. "It turned out he'd been taking bribes all along, a little at a time. He'd tip off a raid, slow down a hot call, make sure there was a way out for one of his people.... And I didn't have a clue. I'd never suspected it for a second." She shook her head, disgusted all over again at both of them.

"You loved him." Nick's voice was inflectionless.

She didn't try to read his expression. "That, and I trusted him." Which she'd learned were two different things. Love came from the heart, trust straight from the gut. And after Terry, she'd stopped believing in both of them, by far preferring less complicated, safer things like desire and companionship.

Nerves stirring at the thought that those, too, had gotten complicated for her, she continued, "It got worse, though, because there weren't just payoffs to him… some were made to look like they had gone to me." She took a deep breath as his eyes darkened. "And they coincided with times the evidence failed in big investigations."

"Failed?"

"Sometimes science isn't…well, a science. Tests can bomb. Contamination can make good-looking evidence useless. More, it's not an analyst's job to connect the dots, at least it wasn't back in the big city." In Bear Claw, they were far more involved in the actual cases. "We gave our findings to the detectives and they took it from there. But sometimes the way an analyst writes a report can influence what the cops take away from it. There were questions." Accusations. Dark looks in the hallway and whispers around every corner.

"You didn't do it." It wasn't a question.

"Of course not. I'm here, aren't I?" Irritation flashed quick and bright. "Matt wouldn't have hired me if I had messed with evidence."

"That wasn't what I meant." A grim-faced Nick looked like he was slowly simmering now, like he wanted to take a piece out of Terry.

She could relate, even appreciate the sentiment, but she couldn't deal with the way it made her want to lean into him, lean on him. Not when they were sitting at her breakfast bar and she'd just polished off his orange chicken and her second glass of wine.

So she said simply, "No. I didn't do it. Terry was working with two other guys in the department—a detective and an analyst. They had been covering for each other for years, and when Terry…died…" Why did she still have to pause before saying that? "Well, when things started coming out, they went into damage-control mode and shifted things around to make it look like Terry and I were working together as a team, that there wasn't anybody else involved. They almost got away with it, too."

She didn't want to remember the suspicious looks, the men and women she'd considered friends avoiding her eyes in the halls, as if they were afraid they might catch crooked copping.

"Anyway, Internal Affairs investigated, of course, but Terry's partners were very good at covering their tracks. Meanwhile, the defense attorneys were dog piling on our old cases, trying to get everything I had ever touched thrown out." That had been the worst, thinking of all those criminals getting a pass because of something she hadn't even done, something only her parents believed her innocent of. Swallowing hard, she made herself keep going. "I got to keep my job because of my father—not just because he was the chief's fishing buddy, but because of his not-too-subtle hints that we would sue if they fired me outright. So they didn't. They turfed me to admin." Another basement, this one with no posters, no friends, at a time when she had badly needed them. "Things were…difficult."

"Hello, understatement," Nick said matter-of-factly, as if he realized she didn't want sympathy right now, couldn't have handled it.

He was right, of course. It had been hell, and she had been sorely tempted to give up, walk out, go hide somewhere while the investigation ran its course. But she had refused to blacken her father's reputation any further, refused to let her mother see her quit. So she stuck it out, even though some days it had taken everything she had just to get out of bed and go to work.

She hesitated, knowing it'd be safer if she just stuck with the facts and let him read what he wanted to—or didn't want to—between the lines. There was a new tension in the air, though, one that reminded her of earlier on the roof, making this feel more important than she had expected, even though their boundary lines had been drawn.

Aware that he was waiting, fiddling a little with one of the fortune cookies that had come with their meal, she finally said, "It was awful. I hated going to work, hated waking up in the morning and knowing I was going to have to sit through another day of looks and whispers, and probably more questions from IA." She paused. "I didn't get to grieve, really, because I didn't just lose Terry, I lost all the good memories of him and the two of us together. It had all been lies, after all. When we were together, he was the perfect husband, the perfect partner...but the rest of the time he was someone else. Not just a cop—I get that they need to have a poker face, maybe more than one—but a crooked cop. How many roles was he playing?"

Nick shifted. "I don't—"

"I used to wonder whether that was part of why he married me," she said, not letting him finish. Not wanting to talk about the parallels between him and Terry right now. "Whether I was part of him looking respectable. Heck, they were talking about him being chief someday."

"Sounds like you weren't the only one he fooled."

She nodded, swallowing past the sudden lump in her throat. "True enough. But I was the one closest to him. At least I thought I was." And how wrong she had been. "When IA finally cracked the case, it turned out there had been other women, too. Classy women, singles who'd thought he was a businessman of some sort. He used them for cover, for sex, for…hell, I don't know. He used them, used me, used all of us. He was gone, though, which meant I never got to blame him for it, not really. And by the time IA figured it all out and busted his real partners, the damage was done. The department was in shambles, the crime lab and all its cases broken open…and even though I'd been cleared, most everybody still treated me like it was my fault. Like I should've seen what was going on with Terry, should've blown the whistle myself."

And maybe they were right.

"So you left."

"At least my father's name was cleared." Though it hadn't really mattered in the end, as her parents had left town soon after she did, driving a leased RV and claiming they'd always wanted to see the rest of the lower forty-eight. "But, yeah, I left. I moved, got paid a ridiculous amount to manage a paternity testing lab, and hid out, licking my wounds. It took six months before I started waking up, a year before I was bored senseless." With the work, the people, the city. "And now I'm here."

She looked around her apartment, which she'd chosen for its view of the skyline and the distant ski slopes, invisible now in the darkness but gorgeous from dawn to dusk. Just now, the city lights twinkled like a giant stretch of holiday lights, making her think of all the people out there who lived in Bear Claw, depended on it being as safe as the cops could make it.

"It's a good place," he agreed, though they both knew he meant a good place for her, not him.

"You're right," she said, forcing aside the pang. "It's a good place, and I want to stay here. I'm grateful that Matt gave me the chance, grateful that Alyssa and the others not only okayed my hiring, they've embraced me, made me one of their own. Even this." Her gesture encompassed Nick, then the street below. "I know they're hoping the Investor will come after me, and I don't mind. But it matters that everybody is being so protective of me. Even you."

The last two words hung there for a moment, suddenly seeming to mean more than she'd intended.

"Jenn…" he began, then trailed off.

"It's okay," she said too quickly. "You don't have to say anything—it's been over for a long time, and for the most part, I've moved on. I guess I wanted you to know about Terry so you'd understand why I'm so attached to Bear Claw…and why it bothers me to see you change from one minute to the next, putting on different faces depending on who you're dealing with."

He reached out and took her hand in a clasp that sent a rush of heat through her body. His eyes were a deep, vivid blue, his hair free now of its tieback, falling loose to his shoulders in thick waves, his expression a mix of anger and regret. "I'm sorry as hell that you had to go through that. Part of me wishes he hadn't died, because then I could track him down and take some payback out of his worthless skin."

It shouldn't have made her feel better to picture it, to know that he would have beaten up Terry if he could.

"Don't worry about it," she said, not letting herself acknowledge the little lift beneath her heart. "What's past is past, and it made me the person I am today, put me in the place I'm in right now. Besides, this is me, remember? I can handle myself. Except maybe when it comes to homicidal drug lords—then I'm going to need your help."

"You've got it. Hell, you can have whatever I can give you, Jenn. I just wish…"

"Yeah," she said as that little moment of almost happiness slipped away, lost to the reality of the situation. "Me, too." She wished she wasn't stuck here with him, trying to pretend that everything was okay when they both knew it wasn't. She wished she could remember the Investor's face, wished this was already over, that he was in jail and she could go back to making a life for herself, here in Bear Claw. Alone.

Suddenly unable to sit still any longer, she rose and started clearing the cartons from their dinner. "Well, it's getting late." Not that she was tired. She just didn't want to sit out there with him anymore, wishing for the impossible.

"Yeah. I'll probably work for a bit, then turn in." He didn't call her on the cowardice, though the look in his eyes said they both knew what was going on.

She hesitated, glancing at the couch and remembering all too well that he didn't fit on it. Not horizontally, anyway.

Following her gaze, he lifted a shoulder. "It'll be fine."

"You'll be in agony."

"I'll crash on the floor."

"Like I said." She looked back at the bedroom, felt her head spin a little and knew the second glass of wine had caught up with her. "We could share. Platonic. Separate blankets. That sort of thing."

"Jenn…" He stared at her, but he didn't say no.

"We're both adults, and I'd say we've covered a lot of ground today." Had she really woken up in the mountains? God, that seemed like forever ago. Since then, he had saved her, kissed her, pushed her away, apologized and promised to protect her. Was it any surprise she was having trouble walking away from him now?

That, and she was a little drunk. Drunk enough that she didn't stop herself from saying, "Please? I really don't want to be alone tonight."

Chapter Nine

Nick's pause was long and telling, so long that Jenn knew he was trying to find the right words to turn her down.

Flushing, she looked away. "Guess not, huh? Well, you're probably right, forget I asked. Lord knows we don't have much of a track record when it comes to platonic anything."

"Okay."

She turned back.

"I'll take half the bed. Assuming the offer's still open."

She wasn't sure which was worse—the thud of her pulse at his agreement or the quick sting of disappointment at the implication that he could do platonic when it came to her. Then again, he'd already made it plenty clear that whatever he felt for her, it wasn't enough to overcome his discipline and better sense.

Be grateful, she told herself. *One of us needs to be rational here.* She knew darn well that it wasn't fair to be annoyed by his self-control when she didn't really want to start things back up. Frustration kicked, not aimed at him this time, but at herself. She was feeling weak, and knew it. Which meant she should take the darn couch.

"The offer's still open," she said instead. "And thank you."

Fool me once...

They dealt with the logistics in a companionable if somewhat strained silence, using the bathroom, wearing far too many clothes and pulling out extra blankets so they could each have their own sets and wouldn't touch in the night. Wouldn't cuddle.

Ten minutes later, he clicked off the lights, leaving them in the darkness, rolled up side by side.

"Good night," she said softly, not letting herself dwell on how odd it was to lie there without touching him, without kissing him.

"'Night, Jenn. Sleep well."

She might've laughed at the thought, but as she curled up in her blanket nest, even though she was careful not to touch him, his body heat seeped into her, along with the reality of his presence and the steady breathing that said he wasn't asleep, not yet. And she felt herself relaxing toward sleep when she wouldn't have thought it possible.

They had been apart far more days than they'd been together, yet in some ways it felt as if he'd never left. She was instantly easy with him there, warm and relaxed beneath the buzz of desire. It was that buzz, though, that said things weren't like they used to be. She wasn't sated, hadn't been thoroughly loved. And wouldn't be.

He was there, though, protecting her, making her feel safe. And, yeah, maybe that safety was an illusion, but she would cling to the pretense for right now, because that was far more comforting than the knowledge that somewhere outside, beyond the safe perimeter, the Investor was planning to kill her.

Don't think about it, she told herself. And she wouldn't, she decided. Instead, she would think about the warm, solid bulk beside her, and the fact that they understood each other a little better now than before. For better or worse.

Closing her eyes, she let herself be lulled by his steady breathing, the gentle wine-spin of the room and the knowledge that, at least for tonight, she wasn't alone.

NICK AWOKE NEAR DAWN, when the false light was just beginning to outline the mountains and the city was still mostly asleep.

Jenn, too, was still slumbering, her face soft, her breathing a steady rise and fall beneath her blanket cocoon. She was facing him, had her hands curled beneath her chin, and she looked like nothing he'd ever seen before in his life.

She damn near took his breath away.

It wasn't just that she was beautiful, though he'd noticed that right away when they'd first met. He was a Lang male, after all, and was therefore programmed to appreciate the hell out of a curvy body, along with high cheekbones, a wide and mobile mouth, and eyes so expressive that they practically had a language of their own, though not one he always understood. So, yeah, she was gorgeous. But she was so much more than that.

She had a delicately angled jaw that could go firm and stubborn on a moment's notice, a spine that walked her into crime scene after crime scene even though they gave her nightmares she wouldn't admit to, and narrow, fine-boned hands that could work near miracles with soil samples…as well as his body.

It was those other things that had caught and held him, and had made him do dumb things. Like dumping her without an explanation. Like thinking he could see her almost every day without wanting her. Like sleeping with her and promising celibacy and pretending it wouldn't be torture.

That was what she needed from him, though. And so he would give it to her.

Somehow.

"You're staring," she said without opening her eyes. Hell, without doing anything that would've warned him she was awake. But that was his Jenn, always full of surprises.

Only she wasn't his Jenn.

Leave it alone, he told himself. Last night she had been buzzed, stressed and vulnerable, and she had asked him to help her out as part of the backward friendship they seemed to be developing. There was no way he should complicate things further under the circumstances.

She's not buzzed now, his inner devil reminded him; that part of him didn't care about anything more than the heat that had settled low in his gut, and the way his chest had tightened when he'd thought about her being his woman.

Her eyes opened, blurry with sleep but clearing as she looked at him, and her expression went softly quizzical. "Who are you right now?"

The question hit hard, not just because she looked into his face and needed to ask, but he didn't have an answer. He wanted to think he was entirely himself unless he chose to become one of the others—Bad Cop, Good Cop, the Underling…the list went on and on. Now, though, he wondered whether he needed to add another: the Lover. Because as he lay there looking into her eyes, there was nothing he wanted more than to know that he would be able to do the same thing tomorrow, the next day and the next.

He wanted to touch her, kiss her, lose himself in her, write her some damn poetry and recite it over a picnic in the state park. Which was how he knew that this wasn't him, couldn't be him. It had to be another role.

"My parents own a theater in New York City." He surprised himself by saying it, but at least it wasn't poetry. "It's several 'offs' away from Broadway, but it's in a good neighborhood and has a strong local following, good word of mouth. Enough that ticket sales have stayed pretty reliable, even now. And back when I was a kid…" He grinned. "It was a pretty great way to grow up, doing stuff behind the scenes, playing bit parts, seeing that world from the wings."

He didn't know why he was telling her all this. Or maybe he did and he didn't want to admit it.

She had gone utterly still. Instead of asking what he was getting at, though, she said, "You were on the stage?"

"We all were—me, my older brother, Stephen, my younger sister, Caroline. Whenever the script called for a 'ragamuffin cameo'—that's what my mother called it—we would step in. Even our dog, Max, made it out there a few times. My mother worked sometimes, but she mostly acted as the stage manager-slash-stage mom, keeping everything up and running. My dad usually directed, though sometimes they would switch it up and she would direct while he managed." He paused. "Looking back, I think that mostly happened when she wanted to remind him that he didn't run the universe. Let's just say, she was a better director than he was stage manager. Probably still is. They have a core group of actors and stage crew, most of them relatives. Aunts, uncles, cousins, nieces, nephews, the works."

Even now, the memories made him grin. More, they reminded him that he should really call home. Maybe visit. It had been too long.

Jenn shook her head. "That sounds…like nothing I can really imagine. Or maybe something I would've imagined. You know, the only child of parents who both worked full-time plus imagining what it would be like to be surrounded by family."

"It rocked." He propped his head on his hand, so he was lying on his side, facing her fully. "I won't pretend there weren't fights. There were, of course. Big, loud ones that sent everybody off in opposite directions, cursing up a storm. Nobody does drama like actors, after all." He lifted a shoulder. "It always blew over, though, or got worked out. We're a tight group. Were a tight group," he corrected, "until I broke the mold and went cop."

"They didn't like the idea?"

"They worried about me." They still did, he knew, and didn't really believe he was happy being Cool Uncle Nick. "And, yeah, they would've liked to keep me in the fold. My brother and sister both stayed in acting. Callie ended up in L.A., but Stephen circled back to the theater after doing some commercial work. Now it's his kids playing the bit parts." He grinned, remembering the last bunch of playbills he'd gotten, along with a wistful tug. Yeah, he really needed to visit. Maybe when this case was over, he could take a few weeks in New York before he went back down south.

The thought of his time in Bear Claw being over brought a twinge, though, and made him very aware of the woman lying beside him, studying him with thoughtful eyes. "That's it, isn't it? You're acting."

"Now? Nope. What you see is what you get." And that was the God's honest truth.

But she shook her head. "That's not what I'm talking about. I mean, it is, but it isn't."

"I'm not following you." He couldn't read her expression, except to know that whatever was going on inside her head, it was important to her. More, it put a faint shimmy in the pit of his stomach, one that said it might be important to him, too.

Don't go there. His blood warmed, though, at the look in her eyes.

"Sorry." She reached out as if to touch him, but drew back before she made contact. The move made him very aware that they were lying in bed together, their bodies sharing warmth even through the blankets separating them. "Forget it."

"Don't stop now."

She rolled onto her side and propped up her head on a hand so they were facing each other, positions mirrored, their bodies separated only by a few layers of cloth. "After Terry died and everything started coming out, hindsight being twenty-twenty, I realized just how much of what I thought we'd had together had been a lie. I'm not even sure he did it consciously all the time, or if he was just a natural manipulator."

"That's a good way of describing lots of actors," he

said, not sure how to defend himself, or if he ought to even try. There was more of a similarity there than he wanted to know, especially lying in bed beside her.

"You're not the same as him, though, are you?" she said, watching him intently. "You know when you're doing it, and you do it on purpose. When you're talking to nice little old lady witnesses, you're the Sweet Nice Officer. With thugs, you're the Tough Cop, maybe even the I'm Badder Than You guy. With a semi-smart perp like Slider, you're all business with an edge of don't-mess-with-me.... Yet with other cops there's none of that tough-guy stuff. You listen to them, make them feel important." She paused. "Those are roles, aren't they? They're not really you."

They're all me, he almost said. That would've been too easy, though, and it wouldn't have been the truth. So instead, he went with the harder reality. "I'm that person in the moment, I guess. I'm thinking like him, acting like him, reacting like him...but, yeah. Part of me knows it's a role. At least here."

"But not undercover."

She saw it. Of course she would see it. He nodded. "That's different. When I'm under, I *am* the guy. I eat, sleep, breathe him. Call it method acting, call it being a really damn good undercover cop, whatever. That can't be a role. For the duration, it has to be me." He'd seen agents blow their covers, had nearly done it himself once or twice, early on. That had been a hell of a wakeup call, showing him all too clearly what could happen when an op went to hell.

Yeah, maybe that had been the real beginning of the end, the point where he'd started pulling away from Stacia and the kids. "I guess that maybe I played a role at home back then, too, acting like the sort of husband I wanted to be, and not really realizing until way too late that I was shutting out Stacia and the boys in the process."

He thought how it should've been strange, lying there in Jenn's bed—a bed where they'd made love as many ways as possible, from raucous to tender—talking about their exes. Yet somehow it seemed right. Right, yet unnerving, because he didn't remember the last time he'd talked like this to anyone. He was close with his family, buddies with Tucker and a few guys back in Florida, but even with them, there were boundaries. And with women, he never even came close.

With Jenn, though, it was different. It was natural, comfortable, yet uncomfortable at the same time. Which was just one of many reasons he hadn't been able to make himself walk away for real. Not six weeks ago when he should've made a clean break, and not now, when he knew damn well he should leave her bed before he got drawn any deeper than he already was.

He didn't move, though; he couldn't. Not with her a scant couple of feet away from him, staring at him as if she were seeing him for the first time…or maybe understanding him more than she had before, and liking what she saw.

He cleared his throat. "I'm still the same guy I was yesterday, the same guy I was six weeks ago. Nothing's changed."

"Maybe not for you, but it has for me."

"Jenn…" he began, levering himself up so he rose above her, looked down at her, only then realizing how dangerous a position he'd put himself in. With her eyes still a little drowsy with sleep and her hair fanned out on her pillow, she looked soft and approachable, and so damn sexy it made him ache. He couldn't go there, though, couldn't mess up the new understanding— maybe even friendship—they were starting to build. So he said simply, "I'm myself when I'm with you. I hope you can believe that."

"I can. I do." She lifted a hand to cup his stubble-roughened cheek. "I trust you, Nick. More than I probably should." Her eyes darkened. "And the thing is, I get it now, why you broke things off, and even maybe why you were a jerk about it. You were right, too—I was starting to get in way deeper than either of us meant to go."

His mouth dried to dust. "Yeah. Me, too."

"But that's not a problem now, is it? We understand each other better now, understand the situation. And what's more, I get that you're nothing like Terry. You're you."

His pulse kicked up a notch. "What are you saying?"

Her lips curved faintly. "I'm saying that you're in my bed, we're safely tucked away together and we both want each other. It's not exactly a love nest buried in the forest, but I think we can make do. More, I think we should try again with the no-strings affair, this time with both of us knowing exactly where we stand." She paused, lips curving. "So, what do you say, Detective? Are you interested?"

JENN HADN'T THOUGHT SHE WOULD be worried about his answer—there was no questioning the chemistry, and he'd mostly held back because he hadn't wanted to hurt her, which wasn't an issue now. But when he hesitated, searching her eyes, nerves sparked deep inside her, warning that she wanted this, wanted him, far more than was wise.

"Strictly casual," she said, as much to herself as to him. "We both know the ground rules for real this time, and the reasons for them." Taking a breath, she went for broke. "There won't be a future for us. I get that now, deep down inside. But that doesn't mean there can't be a now...and I'd hate to have you leave here when this is all over, and know we could've had this time together."

It would hurt when he left...but she thought it would hurt worse if he left without them having acted on all the feelings that had broken through over the past two days. She was seeing him in a different light now, understanding him in new ways.

And, smart or not, she liked the guy she was getting to know. She liked him very much.

"Ah, Jenny..." he said, and her stomach tightened at the nickname he'd only ever used when they'd made love. Before she said anything, he added, "I keep telling myself to walk away." His eyes, though, kindled on hers.

Heat flared in her bloodstream. "Looks like you're still here."

He leaned over her, bracing one arm beside her so he was bracketing her, surrounding her yet not touching. "I'll be damned if I can make myself stay away from you. Not even when I tell myself it'd probably be better for both of us."

"That's because you know you're wrong. *This* is better." She wrapped her fingers around his wrist, holding him over her, drawing him close and inviting him in.

With a low, reverent curse, he bent to her, covering her lightly with his body as their faces aligned for a kiss. "Yeah," he rasped softly. "This is better. This is damn near everything right now—I can't think of anything else, can't care about anything else. Except you."

The heat became a burn, the nerves a churn of excitement that rode low in her belly. "Then take me," she whispered against his lips. "We've got the time, here and now, and this doesn't have to change anything we don't want it to."

And if that thought set off faint warnings inside her, she was the only one who needed to know, the only one who *could* know, because just then, Nick kissed her and the rest of the world ceased to exist.

His lips covered hers and he swallowed her gasp as he took things deep and dark in an instant. Sparks detonated inside her along with a sharp yearning and an inner whisper of, *Yes. Oh, yes.*

It felt as if it had been forever since they'd last been together, yet at the same time the weeks telescoped to nothing and it was like they'd never been apart. She knew his taste—sharp, exciting and purely male—and she knew the solid warmth of his body on hers as he shoved the clinging blankets aside and came down on top of her, pressing her into the mattress. Yet there was also a new ache inside her, brittle and poignant, that said she needed to take what she could right now, not knowing if there would be another opportunity.

Before, some part of her had believed—despite everything they'd said to each other about casual and no-strings—that they were starting something. Now she knew better. But instead of that making her sad or panicky, she found herself storing up the sensations, reveling in them and loving the fact that she was getting at least one more chance to feel the way he made her feel.

This, she thought as she arched beneath him and

ran her hands up his back. This was what she needed, what she wanted. Nick had saved her, protected her, come clean to her, and now he was loving her the best he could. And that was magic.

"Ah, Jenny," he said in a voice rough with passion. He nuzzled the side of her neck, kissed the soft spot that made her shiver. "I never stopped thinking about this. I tried, but I couldn't do it."

"You don't have to." And she wouldn't think about the inevitable ending.

Instead, she thought about the way her legs curved around his hips, aligning their bodies through the clothes they had slept in—yoga pants and a scoop-neck sleep shirt for her, boxers and a Miami P.D. T-shirt for him. She took in the warmth of his breath against her ear, the gentle, inciting play of his fingers along the side of one breast and then inward, to send spirals of pleasure racing through her. She tasted him, loved the way he surrounded her and filled her senses, the way her fingers trembled as she pulled his shirt up and off, then splayed her fingers across his strong muscular back. She reveled in his rough impatience as he shucked off his boxers and went to work on her clothes.

And then, thank God, she couldn't think at all, because they were both naked, pressed skin to skin, with his mouth on hers, their hands racing to find and claim flesh and sensation and their bodies trapping the thick length of his erection between them.

She arched against him, riding that hard ridge of flesh and the pounding ache deep inside her. He groaned and surged against her, his breathing hard, his kisses ardent.

There was no need for more foreplay—in a way, all

of yesterday and the weeks before had been leading them up to this point, this moment. The knowledge warmed her as he rolled away and reached for the nightstand, where she'd taken to keeping condoms when he'd been living there.

A pang of sweet pain came from the sound of the drawer, which she hadn't opened since their breakup. She banished the sadness, though. *Not now. Not today.*

Instead, she reveled in the hot press of his body next to hers, the exciting *crinkle-snap* of the condom and the burn of desire as he rolled back to her, into her arms and up against her body. He paused there, looking down at her with such intensity that she almost looked away, afraid he would see too much in her, or that she would see too much in him. She met his eyes, met his stare, and forced her lips to curve. "Hey," she said softly. "Welcome back."

It wasn't what she really wanted to say, wasn't half of what was in her heart, but it seemed safest that way.

"Jenny," he rasped again, and the passion in his face punched a fist of heat through her body.

She reached up to draw him closer, to kiss him and whisper in his ear, "I'm here, Detective. Right here with you."

His groan was rough with need but his hands were gentle on her hips, her center, as he positioned himself at the entrance to her body and then slid gently, oh, so gently, home. He filled her, pressing into her and surrounding her with his big body, his kisses, the touch of his forehead against hers.

Tears stung her eyelids but she didn't let them free. Instead, she wrapped herself around him, tucked her face into the crook of his neck and held on tight as he began to move, slowly at first, but with building intensity.

They'd had sex before, made love before, and everything in between. This time was different, though. There was a new intensity, a new poignancy and a deep, burning heat that said yes, this was right. This was how things were supposed to be between them.

Jenn closed her eyes and gave herself over to the sensations. Her body moved beneath his, against his, taking his thrusts and driving him onward, urging him faster, harder. He said her name, over and over again like an exultant chant that went straight to her heart and sent the heat ever higher, until it spiraled up to a sharp, bright orgasm that caught her by surprise.

She cried out and arched against him, felt him shudder as her body closed around him with sensuous intent. He held out two more strokes and then a third, and then stiffened against her and groaned deep within his chest as his hips jerked against her, into her.

He held himself still, braced with the pleasure of their joining, his face etched with his release. Then, when it was over, he eased down atop her and kissed her deeply, never leaving her body. In fact, he remained semi-hard, as if they had only taken the edge off the desire he'd been repressing for so long. "Again," he said, voice thick. "More."

She didn't say anything; she didn't have the words. She just rose over him, kissed him and made love to him. *Again,* her body said for her. *More.* They couldn't get enough of each other, couldn't leave each other, could only kiss and twine together, and find over and over again the things they had left behind. And somewhere in the middle of it all, the sense of a ticking clock fell away from her, leaving her spent, relaxed and excited all at once.

Here and now was all that mattered. All that could matter.

But then, later, as she lay there, replete and boneless, and wishing she could pretend the world outside didn't exist, it intruded rudely.

Her cell phone rang. Then Nick's.

Their eyes met and the warmth fell away, lost in a quick chill.

"Something's happened with the case," she said, reaching for her cell as he made a grab for his pants. "This is Jenn," she said into the receiver.

"It's Alyssa. There's been another murder...and I think you and Nick should see this."

Chapter Ten

Jerome Bentley—street name Axe, a former Ghost Militiaman who had slipped through the police crackdown several months earlier and gone into hiding—hadn't died easily. He'd gone down fighting, in fact, as evidenced by the spatter on the walls, the busted-up chair and the tipped-over desk.

He'd gone down eventually, though. And that was when the Investor had gotten to work on him, slicing and prodding, burning and slivering until he'd wrung out whatever information he'd been seeking. Then he'd made the final, fatal wound, a ghastly slow one that left Bentley bleeding out and utterly helpless, watching his killer clean his borrowed tools—kitchen knives, needle-nose pliers and screwdrivers—and meticulously arrange them on a set of torn-down curtains.

The Investor had wiped the weapons down with bleach and hadn't taken anything from the apartment. Hadn't left anything behind, either, at least not as far as the cops could tell.

Forty-eight hours after she and Nick had first been called to the Bentley scene, as Jenn bent over a stereomicroscope, looking at the contents of the victim's pockets, she couldn't stop thinking that the Investor was too good at this, too meticulous. How could they catch a man who didn't make a mistake?

What went wrong inside someone's brain, allowing them to do something like this?

And, more, what would it come down to, when she was the only thing keeping him in the city? Slider had said the Investor wouldn't leave without taking care of her. What if he had found what he was looking for? What if she was next on his list?

"You're safe in here," she reminded herself. "There are cops watching the stairs and teams watching the apartment." It wasn't as if she was going home alone, either. Nick would be with her, just like he'd gone with her the past two nights, protecting her, keeping watch over her, chatting with her as they ate takeout. And, when the lights went out, making love to her long into the night.

Lips curving, she said, "Note to self—get more burgers." Takeout was getting old, and she thought they could handle cooking together without it feeling too homey this time. They were sticking to the rules, after all, and enjoying the ride while it lasted. And if she remembered to buy burgers, she would remember to get more condoms, too.

"Talking to yourself?" Gigi asked from the other side of the room, where she was working on the blood-stained curtain, checking to see if all of the blood had come from the victim, or if they had gotten lucky with a second donor, possibly their killer.

"Reminding myself not to freak out," Jenn said, going with a partial truth. "I need to keep telling myself that I'm as safe here as I'd be anywhere." Okay, so maybe that wasn't true—she could've been up at the safe house in the woods, or away on an island somewhere. So she added, "Anywhere that I can be involved in the case, that is."

Whether or not she had needed the reminder, it drained the warmth that had come from thoughts of Nick, replacing it with the chill of knowing that outside the walls of the P.D. there was a man who wanted her dead, who had already killed at least five people himself and who had gained a taste for bloody, vicious torture.

She shivered and reached for the fleece jacket she had slung over the back of her chair.

"You could bail," Gigi said. "Seriously."

"No, I can't. Seriously." She wanted this—not just the job, but a part in nailing the Investor. Glancing over at Gigi, she asked, "You getting anywhere over there?"

"Nada. The little DNA that wasn't degraded beyond recovery by the bleach has all come back as belonging to Bentley. This guy is a damned ghost."

"No, he's most definitely not," Jenn said sharply. "Trust me, I had the bruises to prove it."

Gigi looked contrite. "Sorry."

"No, I'm the one who's sorry. Didn't mean to snap, I'm just frustrated." She paused. "Angry, too. And scared."

It was the first time she'd really said it out loud. Always before, she'd put on the tough face in front of the others. Even with Nick, she needed to be strong, knowing that he would just as soon send her back up into the mountains until the case was over. More, she didn't dare bring up the idea of using herself as bait again, even though it was getting increasingly obvious that needed to be their next move. Which scared the hell out of her, though she thought she was hiding it well.

With Gigi, though, she could say it and know it wouldn't go any further. The other woman knew what it meant to persevere in the face of danger. She had done it when the Investor first appeared on the scene, back when the Militia had been strong and its members had targeted her. She'd made it through with Matt's help, and his love. Jenn hoped she could do the same with Nick's help, though not his love.

What they had was enough. He was giving her his strength, the illusion of safety and a break from being alone. More, she was finally letting go of Terry—not the memory or the grief, but the anger and shame that had come after. That was gone now, in the past, and she was starting a new life in a new city that she loved, with good friends who cared about her.

That would be enough for her. It needed to be enough.

"You'd be an idiot not to be scared," Gigi said bluntly. "Fear is going to keep you careful, and that's going to keep you alive." She paused, lips curving slightly. "That, and Nick. Things seem to be going well between you two…not that I'm prying or anything."

"Sure you are." And she was also changing the subject, which Jenn appreciated. Not because her safety wasn't important, but there wasn't anything more they could do about it just now. They were doing everything they could to solve the case…they just needed that *aha* moment, the key puzzle piece that brought everything falling into place.

"We're just enjoying each other," she said after a moment. "It's like before, but with better communication." And even better sex, though that shouldn't have been possible. But where what they'd had before had been blazing hot, what they had now came with an added layer of tenderness that was new, and thoroughly addictive.

She didn't mention that, though. First, because that was getting into TMI territory, and second because it would only encourage her friend, who thoroughly approved of the way Nick had moved back in and taken over Jenn's nighttime protection. Gigi had also sighed over the way he walked her down to the lab in the morning and kissed her goodbye, then came back down for her at the end of the day to kiss her hello once more.

Not that Jenn was complaining. She just wasn't reading anything into it this time.

"You know," Gigi said as she returned her attention to the bloodstained curtain, "I wasn't planning on staying in Bear Claw when I first got here. I was just in it for the experience, and to impress my bosses enough to get me into the SWAT program. If anyone had hinted that I'd be making this my home base, I would've laughed my butt off."

"Gigi…" Jenn began, but then trailed off, because what was there to say? There were parallels, it was true. Matt had been entrenched in his job as head ranger high up in the mountains, Gigi on the fast track to an exciting new job, and they had both wound up changing their tangents to meet halfway. Which was great for them, but didn't mean it would work for everyone, or even that she should try. "Look, seriously, what Nick and I have going right now is working for us. We're having fun—no strings, no guilt, just two people who enjoy the hell out of each other."

"And you're okay with that?"

"I really am. Not every relationship is meant to last forever."

"What if this one is, and you're both just being stubborn?"

"It's not about being stubborn, it's about being honest. He does what he does, and I do what I do, and the two really can't meet in the middle."

"But—"

"Just let it go, okay?" Jenn asked quietly when her throat tightened. "Please?" The sudden emotion didn't come from grief. It came from knowing that what she wanted—what she thought they both wanted, on some level—just wasn't possible.

"Of course. I'm sorry. I said I wasn't going to pry and I did it, anyway, didn't I?"

Jenn summoned a smile. "What are friends for?"

"Still. Not cool. Buy you lunch to make up for it?"

"Only if we can get it delivered." Sigh. More take-out. But if an overdose of MSG was the worst thing that happened to her while she was on lab-and-house arrest, she would count herself very lucky.

They went back to their tasks. Jenn was going through the contents of a dead man's pockets. She had already fingerprinted the coins and tested them for trace, had earmarked a used napkin for DNA and other chemical analyses, and now was working on the last item: a wadded, fibrous mess that had looked like another napkin at first, but had turned out to be a piece of paper that had been through the laundry at least once.

It was probably nothing, of course—at least ninety percent of the so-called evidence they collected turned out to be useless—but she enjoyed the challenge of re-constructing printed pieces almost as much as she got turned-on by soil samples. She loved the tricky stuff, the puzzles that needed the human factor to solve it, rather than expensive machines.

So far, she had teased the wad flat, keeping it aligned when the fragile pink paper wanted to break along the weakened folds, and used a variety of filters to photograph it under the stereoscope, hoping the indirect lighting and a couple of nifty computer programs she had on hand would help clarify what was left of the ink. The printed lines had remained indistinct, though, which meant it was time to move on to using chemicals to bring out the words on the page.

She thought it was a receipt—the kind that was preprinted, then filled out by hand, though there wasn't any sign of ballpoint ink.

"Probably from a Laundromat," she said to herself, though from his apartment, Bentley hadn't exactly seemed like a dry-clean kind of guy. It was more a reminder not to get her hopes up as she slid the fragile piece of paper into a shallow tray filled with the proper chemicals.

At the same time, though, this was what she loved about the job—that lottery-ticket feeling that came with each new piece of evidence, each bit of progress that made her think *this could be the one*.

"Got something?" Gigi asked without looking up.

"I'm not sure. It's probably nothing, but maybe we'll get lucky for a change." Jenn checked her digital lab timer. "I'll let you know in three…two…one…darn it. Nothing. I'll have to try—" She broke off as shadows darkened on the page, turning into wavy lines, maybe even some words. "Hang on. Hold that thought."

Pulse kicking up a notch, she leaned in, focusing

the optics of the stereoscope more precisely and then, when that didn't do much, going back through the filters she'd tried before. It took a frustrating few minutes for the images to load and the analysis program to do its thing, predicting missing pixels from the surrounding patterns.

When the image came up on her screen, though, it was worth it. "Aha," she breathed. Because this looked as if it might be exactly the sort of break they'd been searching for.

AN HOUR AFTER HE'D GOTTEN Jenn's call of "I think you're going to want to see this," Nick pulled up at the Lazy Joe Ranch in an unmarked and unremarkable pickup truck. He was carrying concealed with Tucker riding shotgun, and they had a dozen good men and women just waiting for the signal to swoop in and take charge of the scene.

Still, though, Nick's blood was pumping as he dropped down from the truck, shoved his hands in the pockets of his jeans and took a look around, playing the part of a local guy looking to rent a storage bay, just like the unit listed on the receipt Jenn had found in Bentley's personal effects.

The Lazy Joe Ranch had probably been lovely at one point, but that would've been a few years ago, and those intervening years hadn't been kind. The main ranch house, which was visible in the middle distance, was missing shingles and had a serious sag to its porch. The outbuildings had weathered from barn-red to a dispirited pinkish color, and one roof wore ragged blue tarps here and there, no doubt covering holes that had been on the "to be repaired" list for a long time.

Nick had parked in an open lot near a row of parallel steel buildings with accordion doors and "For Rent" painted on the short ends. A trailer parked at an angle in the lot had a fat hound sleeping beside the steps and "Office" painted on the door. On the other side of the trailer were a half-dozen round pens, where three winter-fluffed horses picked at wisps of hay and poked at saddles slung over the rails. A sign offered trail rides by the hour.

Nick cast a look back down the driveway, at the wrought-iron sign that arched over the driveway, swinging gently in a fitful breeze and squeaking on its fastenings. "The Lazy Joe, huh?" To be honest, this was the first time he'd really felt he was out in the West, far from his usual home base.

"Rumor has it that the prior owner named it after her ex-husband," Tucker said. "She sold out about five years ago and the current guy, Larry Dent, picked it up on the cheap, planning on turning it into an eco-friendly dude ranch specializing in exotic meats. Ostrich. Buffalo. That sort of thing."

"I take it that didn't work out so well."

"I guess he had some investors who lost their money when the market crashed, and then got in trouble with his suppliers. Add in the droughts we've been having, and even experienced ranchers have been struggling, never mind a start-up." Tucker shrugged. "Dent leased out the land to a local family and went back to the East Coast."

"Looks like the locals have diversified." Nick glanced at a sagging wire fence line that marked off the pasture, where some decent-looking cows—for all that he knew about cows, anyway—were hanging out under a bunch of trees. Then, figuring he was far better off with people than cows, he headed for the office, intent on getting some answers.

The hound raised its head at the men's approach, but greeted them with a tail thump rather than bared teeth. Nick gave it a nod on the way through the door. "Nice to meet you, too."

Tucker's chuckle followed him in.

There was a desk near the door, heaped with papers, the chair behind it empty. A skinny young woman in her late teens sat on a rump-sprung couch farther into the space, frowning down at the clunky laptop. As the men came in, she looked up. "Help you?"

Her voice was polite, but her hand went toward a cushion that lay flat on the sofa, with the sort of instinctive twitch that told Nick that he and Tucker weren't the only ones with concealed weapons.

"Easy there," he said, going on instinct by jettisoning the "local guy looking to rent a locker" act and bringing up Good Cop by flashing the badge out of his pocket. "We're not looking for trouble. We just need some info on one of your renters."

Her eyes got big, but she stood her ground rather than trying to rabbit out the back. "I'm just filling in. Daddy—my father—should be back around six. He got some hours over at the gas station, doing oil changes and stuff. We need the money, and this place isn't exactly raking it in." The look she shot around the Lazy Joe was more weary than anything, but when her eyes came back to Nick, they held a quiet sort of entreaty. "There's trouble, isn't there?"

"I'm afraid so, and we can't wait until he gets back. Can you call him?"

"The boss won't like that." Which, he knew, could mean the loss of those precious hours.

"Sorry, but either you let us into your records and open up this locker—" Nick unfolded a copy of the receipt Jenn had reconstructed and held it out, along with a warrant "—or we call him in to do it for us." When her expression darkened, he added, "We'll keep this as low-key as possible, but we need to do it. The guy who rented the space is dead. Murdered."

"Oh!" Her eyes went wide. "He…oh. Oh, wow. Um. Okay. Wow. Of course." She grabbed the receipt, barely glanced at the warrant, and sat at the desk to rummage in a couple of file-cabinet drawers. She talked the whole time—about how she was taking criminal justice classes at the local community college, and how she wanted to work for the D.A.'s office and maybe put herself through law school. Or maybe she'd be a cop. She hadn't decided yet, but had good grades in everything except Spanish, which really wasn't her thing.

It wasn't a guilty babble, Nick knew. It was more a very human reaction to learning about a death that was only indirectly connected to her, and the relief that it hadn't been worse. And if it reminded him of Jenn's coping strategies when it came to crime scene work, nobody needed to know about it but him, just like nobody needed to know how often he thought about her, and how glad he was that Tucker had vetoed her request to come out to the Lazy Joe with them.

With her safely tucked away at the P.D., he could focus on the job rather than worrying about her.

Two minutes later, he was armed with a carbon copy of the receipt Jenn had found—one year, paid in advance by the victim—along with a pair of bolt cutters and the girl's go-ahead for him and Tucker to cut open Bentley's locker.

With no evidence that the owners of the storage units were involved with the former Ghost Militia, and with nothing hitting their warning instincts, they signaled for the others to close in on the Lazy Joe.

As they arrived, Nick headed for the locker, leaving Tucker to brief the incoming task force members. After a moment, two uniformed officers headed his way, pulling their weapons and gesturing that they would flank the storage space.

Locker twelve was at the end of a row. There were high vents over the door and on the end of the building. The steel construction wasn't nearly so ramshackle as the ranch buildings, but the gray paint and dark green doors seemed ominous against the gunmetal gray sky.

The cattle had moved from their resting spot, drawn by the commotion down in the parking area, maybe. Nick was conscious of their thudding hooves and occasional calls, which made him very aware that he wasn't in Miami anymore. It was rare for him to feel out of place—he could bluff his way through damn near anything—but the openness and Old West feel had him a little off balance, making him think he should be wearing a gun belt and a star-shaped badge.

Not just Good Cop, but Good Cop with a Stetson.

He glanced at the two guys backing him up, got their nods, and set the bolt cutters to the flimsy lock holding the door shut. It snapped off with minimal protest and clattered to the ground. Hearing nothing from inside the locker, Nick inched the garage-type door up a notch and crouched down to sweep his flashlight beneath.

Seeing only a jumble of packing boxes, he straightened and waved to Tucker, who was headed his way across the parking lot with the others behind him. "Looks clear," Nick called.

"Then let's open 'er up."

The green door rolled up a few inches and then stuck with a rusty grating noise, and Nick had to put his shoulder into it. One of his backup stepped forward to help just as it gave a grating *pop* and rolled free, rattling up into its overhead holder. Nick quickly scanned the stacked boxes, empty, along with a couple of bare dollies and a jumble of discarded-looking computer equipment and wires.

But it wasn't the rattle that froze him in place, or the sight of the junk that'd been left behind.

It was the popping noise, and the subsonic whine that followed it.

"Run!" he shouted, spinning and waving the others away. "Take cover!"

He was moving already, heading for open—

Crack-boom! The storage unit detonated with a roar of concussion and flames.

The shock wave slammed into Nick, sent him flying. And all he could think as he slammed face-first into the dirt was, *Should've called the bomb squad and their dogs,* followed by, *Thank Christ Jenn is safe.* Because on the heels of that was the knowledge of what this discovery had to mean: the empty boxes and leftovers suggested that the Investor had found what he'd been looking for. Which meant she was the only thing keeping the criminal mastermind in Bear Claw...and he'd be coming for her soon.

Chapter Eleven

The cruiser Jenn had commandeered rolled into the parking lot of the Lazy Joe just as the storage building blew.

She didn't know if she screamed or not, didn't know if the officer tried to keep her in the cruiser or not, because in the aftermath of the blast, as flames roared and a huge cloud of dark smoke and debris rolled up the alley between the storage buildings, her mind blanked and her body acted without rational thought.

"Nick!" She knew he was down there, knew he would've been the one to open the door.

She was out of the car in an instant, pounding across the parking area. She didn't care about the danger or the fact that she was supposed to stay in the car, wasn't even supposed to be there at all. All she cared about was getting to Nick.

But she couldn't see him, couldn't see anything through the gray-brown clouds and inky smoke.

Her heart raced in her chest and her feet thudded on the hard-packed gravel. Someone shouted her name; someone else made a grab for her. She didn't stop, though, couldn't stop. Then she was inside the cloud, choking and coughing, and feeling the sudden burn of the nearby fire heating the air. "Nick," she shouted. "Nick!"

There was no answer, but when the smoke shifted a little, she caught sight of two shadows off near the edge of the far storage building—one a man down and motionless, crumpled against the dented door, with another man bending over him, then straightening to shout for help in a ragged voice: "Officer down!"

And her heart stopped.

"No!"

The kneeling man's head jerked up; his eyes went wide and angry. "Jenn, what are you—" He bit off the question with a curse. "For heaven's sake, *get back!*"

Nick was angry, but just then she didn't care. All she cared was that he was okay. Her head spun and her legs went watery, and to her utter mortification she realized she was about to pass out. Which wasn't going to help the situation one bit. *Nick's okay,* she told herself. *He's okay. He's not the officer down.* The words went through her like a mantra but did little to steady her.

Be strong, she told herself. Don't wimp out now.

Lungs heaving, she spun and staggered away from the explosion site, suddenly aware that she was out in the open in the middle of chaos, one the Investor had created. What if he was there? Had he set off the explosion? Was he even now closing in on her in the sooty smoke?

Back at the lab, it had seemed imperative that she bring her second discovery—another receipt, this one for Unit Thirteen—out to the site herself when she hadn't been able to get through by phone. Now, though, she realized she was just being stubborn, perhaps fatally so.

She shouldn't have left the lab, shouldn't have bolted out of the cruiser. She had to get back!

A man appeared out of the gritty cloud and she shrank back, nearly turning to run, but then she recognized the officer she'd been sitting with. His eyes were wide and wild, his jaw set, and he grabbed her and hustled her back to the cruiser, shouting "I've got her" over his shoulder.

The next half hour was a blur of rescue vehicles, sirens and shouted orders that Jenn only half heard through the windows of the locked-down cruiser, followed by the dizzying lurch of movement, then more siren sounds as the ambulances pulled away and the cruiser she was riding in followed, rocketing the miles back to the city, leaving the Lazy Joe behind.

She wasn't going back to the lab, though. The officer was taking her to the hospital, following the ambulance that carried Nick.

He'd been hurt. Not as critically as the two officers who'd served as backup, but still hurt enough to agree to an ambulance.

"Nick," she whispered through numb lips, only then realizing that her hands were shaking; all of her was shaking.

"He'll be okay," her driver assured her over his shoulder, and she had the feeling it wasn't the first time he'd said it.

It was the first time she'd really processed it, though, and it was the first time she caught the worry in his eyes when he glanced in the rearview at her. "What about the others?" she made herself ask as the world started to come back into focus around her.

"We'll have to wait and see."

Suddenly feeling very small and self-centered, she sank back in her seat, eyes glued to the ambulance up ahead, with its flashing lights and precious cargo. *Officer down.* It wasn't the first time one of Bear Claw's cops had fallen during the Death Stare case. But, she was forced to admit, it was the first time it had hit so close to home.

Worse, when she followed her escort through the sliding doors into the E.R. waiting room, all the familiar faces turned and locked on her when she walked through the doors.

For a second, she flashed back on the night Terry died.

Back then, before all the bad stuff had come out, she had walked into that hospital waiting room and found all their friends there, all their coworkers, and she'd seen the looks on their faces and she'd known it was real. Up to that point, part of her had thought it was a mistake, that she would get there and Terry would be waiting for her, contrite that she'd been scared. He would hold her and tell her he was fine, that everything was going to be okay.

Only he hadn't been waiting, and things had been far from okay.

Now, the looks were the same. The sudden cold, congealing fear in the pit of her stomach was the same.

Bile pressed at the back of her throat. Sudden panic.

This was partly why she had embraced the safe boredom of the DNA testing lab, partly why she'd made a point of dating normal guys with normal jobs. She hadn't wanted to be here, hadn't wanted to go through this ever again—all those eyes reflecting shock, grief and the pity that said louder than words, *We know you loved him, and we're sorry about what happened.*

How had she forgotten this part? How could she deal with it?

"Jenn." Gigi appeared suddenly in front of her, and took her arm. "Are you okay?"

"I'm…" Jenn saw another woman, a stranger who huddled in a corner chair and blotted at haggard, tear-filled eyes with a napkin while the woman who sat next to her—an older, heavier version of the crying woman—fussed quietly over her with fluttering hands and a sad, worried expression. And although Jenn didn't know either of them, she knew exactly who they were, what they were going through.

The far doors swung open without warning, and everybody in the waiting room jolted and looked toward the doctor who appeared. His scrubs were mostly clean, but Jenn's trained eye picked out the faint spatters above his knees, showing where he'd been wearing a surgical gown.

She swallowed hard, held on to Gigi's hand too tightly, but the surgeon's eyes went to the weeping woman. "Mrs. Trumble?"

Gulping a sob, the woman lurched to her feet, pulling her mother with her. "Jeffrey," she said urgently. "Is he…?"

"He's going to be okay. He came through surgery just fine, and is on his way to recovery right now. You can see him if you want."

"Yes!" Her eyes filled. "Oh, yes. Of course. Oh…"

The surgeon kept talking, describing Trumble's injuries in more depth and reassuring his friends and wife of the prognosis. Jenn only half heard the details, though, because just then the door swung open again and a very familiar figure filled the doorway, stalled there for a moment as he looked around the room. Then blue eyes locked on her, and he headed straight for her.

Nick!

His gaze was dark and hard, reminding her suddenly of the way she'd run into the smoke, looking for him, but she didn't care if he was mad at her, just that he was *there,* on his feet and walking toward her.

He was wearing scrubs, unlaced sneakers she didn't recognize and a dark blue parka marked with BCCPD insignia. His clothing—and undoubtedly his person— had been processed for evidence, forcing him to borrow from the lost and found. Cassie or Alyssa would have taken his clothes, or maybe one of the bomb experts. They would have the first crack at this scene, after all, needing to know what kind of device it had been, how it'd been set off.

But although that corner of her mind was aware of the practicalities—and the chain of evidence—the rest of her focused utterly on the man walking toward her. "Nick," she said softly, the word slipping between her lips almost on a sigh.

"I'll go…" Gigi made a vague gesture. "Somewhere else."

The waiting area was practically a task-force meeting, it was so full of cops and analysts, and she knew she should hold it together, keep it casual. But when he got to her, reached for her, she didn't hesitate for even a second. She went into his arms, first holding on tentatively, afraid to hurt him.

"I'm fine," he said into her hair as he gripped her tightly. "Just knocked around a little."

She exhaled and locked her arms around him, burrowing into him for a moment and just concentrating on breathing. On believing that he was there, that this wasn't Terry all over again.

"I'm sorry," she said after a moment, her words muffled in his chest. "I shouldn't have come out to the ranch, shouldn't have gotten out of the car or run toward you like that. I was just… Well. I shouldn't have done it."

He pulled away slightly to look down at her. "Lesson learned?"

"Absolutely."

"Okay, then." He kissed her forehead…but his expression stayed grim.

A sudden chill slid through her at the realization that he might not be playing a role with her right now, but he wasn't being his whole self, either.

"Come on," he said, tugging her toward the exit. "Tucker said for us to go straight back to your place, get some rest. The night shift has got the case for the next ten hours…. So let's get out of here."

But when he said, "Let's get out of here," what she heard was, *We need to talk.*

AS HE DROVE THEM BACK to Jenn's place, Nick knew he'd let things go too far again, and he had only himself to blame. He'd seen it in her face when she'd come running into the blast zone after him, and he'd felt it in himself when he'd seen her there. Despite both their best intentions, they were in too deep, cared too much. And it was going to hurt like hell when it came time to walk away.

Thing was, as he'd sat waiting for the doctors to agree that he had a damn thick skull and none of the bumps he'd gotten were critical, he'd had some time to think...and even though his usual MO was to cut ties as soon as things started to go too far, he'd already tried that once and they'd both been miserable. So, yeah, it was going to hurt when it came time for him to walk and her to stay behind...but as he'd come out of the treatment area, he'd been halfway convinced that there wasn't any reason to bolt now.

Then he'd seen her face, and he'd known it might not matter what he wanted. She'd gotten an up close and personal look at what it was like to be with a guy like him—and, too late, he remembered that she'd already been in this situation once before, and with the worst possible outcome.

"You're mad at me," she said softly from the faraway-seeming passenger's side of the SUV. "And you're right. I shouldn't have left the lab. I could've put even more people in danger doing that."

"Including yourself," he pointed out, but then shook his head. "I'm not mad at you, Jenn."

"Then what?" When he hesitated, she pressed, "Honesty, remember? No more games."

"Yeah. You're right. Okay, yeah, I'm mad...but not at you. I'm mad at myself." Which was the truth, though not all of it. "I never should've just yanked open the door of the storage unit. We knew there was a chance the Investor had been there. I should've damn well guessed he might wire it to blow."

"He hasn't used explosives before," she pointed out. "And you didn't know there was another unit on the other side." The preliminary report suggested that was where the explosives had been stored.

"Still. I should've been more careful."

"Well, if you're going to take the blame for that, I should blame myself for not having realized right away there were two receipts. If you'd known about number thirteen, you might've found the explosives before anybody got hurt." She swallowed hard.

"There's a big difference between you not being able to get through to us on the phone, and my underestimating the Investor and his men like that."

She shook her head. "You're not a mind reader, Nick. Don't beat yourself up over something that seems obvious in twenty-twenty hindsight."

"I wouldn't be if it was only me. But Trumble's hurt because of me, and it could've been far worse."

"It wasn't. And you heard the doctor. He's going to be okay."

Something twisted inside Nick's chest and, without really meaning to, he reached across and took the hand she'd fisted in her lap. Opening her fingers from their tense grip, he threaded his own between them. "Why are you trying to make me feel better? I saw your face back there in the waiting room, and I have a pretty good idea of what you were going through. Which means that right now you should be telling me to get lost, that you don't want to lose someone else you care about."

She made a muffled sound of protest but didn't pull her hand away.

"That scene back there, it's who I am, how I live." It tore a chunk out of him, but he said it, anyway, voice going rough. "I'm not the kind of guy you want to wait around for, Jenn. I can't be that guy."

They had reached her apartment and sat outside in the driveway, in full view of the two squad cars that were now parked at both ends of the block as a visible deterrent, backing up the hidden surveillance teams. The cruisers underscored the danger, but he left the motor running an extra moment, knowing they needed the time…and maybe hoping she would tell him to get lost, giving him an excuse to shuffle her off to the mountain safe house, where she'd be far safer than she would be here, even with him in her bed.

Hell, even with him on her couch, though he hated the thought. It might be better if they backed off, though. This was getting complicated.

"You're not Terry," she said, quietly but firmly. "I refuse to treat you like you're the same as him."

"There are more similarities than differences."

"Not to me. Not in the ways that matter." She turned to face him, expression suddenly intent. "He wouldn't have been more worried about the other cops than himself, at least not unless somebody was watching, and he wouldn't have been beating himself up over making the wrong call opening up that storage unit. Terry never made mistakes, it was always somebody else's fault. And he sure as hell wouldn't have been trying to talk me out of being with him because I might get hurt."

"Well, I am."

"Too late." She surprised him by leaning across the console to kiss him, tightening her fingers on his as their lips touched, lingered and then softened to a kiss that sent his senses racing, his heartbeat rocketing.

It was too late for him to pull away, had probably been too late for days now, maybe even longer. He was locked in tune with her, and didn't give a crap that the uniforms across the street were probably getting a kick out of the show. He didn't care who knew that they were together—hell, he wanted the others to know, wanted them to keep their hands off his woman.

Only she wasn't his woman.

"I am tonight," she said softly, making him think he'd said it aloud, or maybe that she was reading his mind.

In some dim corner of his brain, he knew he was in just as much danger as she was right now, not from the Investor, but from the explosive heat they created together. He couldn't make himself care, though, couldn't make himself pull away. Instead, he leaned into the kiss and framed her face in his hands. She curled into him, stroking her hands along his arms and back, chasing away the aches wherever she touched, yet kindling another, deeper ache inside him.

He eased the kiss without breaking their embrace, and pressed his forehead to hers, feeling the two of them breathing in sync. "Ask me to come inside with you," he said, voice rough with the passion he wasn't doing a very good job of suppressing. "Ask me to come upstairs to your bed and make love to you."

She smiled against his lips. "Come inside," she said, then kissed him softly. "Come upstairs. Make love to me…and that's not an invitation, Detective. It's an order."

LATER, JENN LAY ON HER SIDE with her head propped on one hand, watching her lover sleep.

Her lover. He was certainly that, and more. She could admit that to herself, if not to him. She cared for him more than she'd meant to, certainly more than anybody she'd been with since Terry. It didn't matter that he would be moving on soon, or that he lived a dangerous life. It only mattered that he was here with her and that he had loved her so well just now.

She needed this. She needed him.

And if she kept telling herself she would be okay when he moved on, eventually it would be the truth... especially if she stepped up and took control of things.

Even sleeping, he looked fierce and capable, and kept one hand on her as if reassuring himself that she was still there. She couldn't keep hiding behind him, though. It was time for her to step up and do what needed to be done, what she probably should have done days ago. Weeks.

Nick would hate it, but she couldn't let that affect her decision. At the same time, she couldn't let him or any of the others keep putting their lives on the line. And she couldn't keep being the weak link in the team, the one who pretended to be capable and self-sufficient but got woozy at crime scenes and needed to be dragged away from bombings. The one who didn't see what was right in front of her and who couldn't remember the things she'd seen.

She needed to do this, not just for her teammates, but for herself.

Refusing to second-guess her decision, she slipped out of the bed, pulled on her robe, dug her cell out of the haphazard pile of clothes on the floor and headed out into the hallway to make the call.

"McDermott here," his voice came on moments later, gruff but alert.

"Tucker, it's Jenn. I'm sorry to call so late, but I've made a decision." She paused, knowing this was the right thing to do, yet still terrified. "I think it's time to bait the trap," she said, forcing her voice to stay steady.

"I want you to leak it to the media that I've remembered what the Investor looks like, and that we expect to have a sketch by morning. Maybe a press conference. Whatever you think will worry the Investor the most."

"You're sure about this." It wasn't a question.

"I want to end this, once and for all, before anyone else gets hurt."

There was a long silence, so long that for a moment she thought he was going to turn her down. But then his sigh echoed along the line, and he said, "Okay, I'll make the calls and get back to you. In the meantime, I'll put out the word to the units guarding your place, and add a few more patrols to the neighborhood." He paused. "Have you talked to Nick about this?"

Her spine straightened even as an uneasy churn settled in her belly. "It's my decision."

"Still, you need to tell him."

"I know. I will." But as she ended the call and sat there for a moment, staring into space and hoping she hadn't just made a huge mistake, she knew she wasn't going to go back into the bedroom and wake him up with the news.

She would find the right moment. Later. Tomorrow. Somehow.

Chapter Twelve

The next morning, Nick awoke to the smell of coffee and bacon. That, and the sizzle of pancakes being flipped, let him know that Jenn was cooking up one of her fabulous breakfasts—she didn't cook often, she had warned him early on, but he had quickly learned that when she did, it was well worth the wait.

His stomach growled because they had skipped dinner the night before, and as he sat up in bed, a few sore spots chimed in, reminding him that yesterday hadn't exactly been smooth sailing. But a check of his phone showed that there weren't any priority-flagged messages and, aside from a few bruises and a couple of pulled muscles, he was feeling good. Damn good, in fact.

He stretched, feeling the slip-slide of her sheets and the give of her soft mattress, along with the whole-body well-being that came from being with her. Especially after yesterday, when he'd thought she'd be done with him in the aftermath of the bombing.

She hadn't dumped him. Instead, she'd accepted him, made love to him. And that was a damned miracle. As for things ending, well, they would deal with that when the time came. There was a small, unfamiliar part of him, though, that wondered whether the end might not be as inevitable as he'd been thinking. She had handled yesterday's events like a true professional and, more, she had comforted him, understood him.

He'd never had that kind of connection with Stacia, hadn't ever believed she could really handle the truth of his day-to-day life.

Granted, Jenn shouldn't have to go through that, especially not after what she'd been through in her marriage. But maybe that was the difference here—she'd been through it, and knew she could survive it. And, more, she knew that a real connection wasn't something they could ignore.

"Listen to yourself," he said, surprised his head had even gone there. "Getting ahead of things, aren't you? We've got a killer to catch first." Hopefully the bastard had slipped up with the bombing, and the techs would have something for them to go on.

Idly thinking he should put in a call to Tucker and get the latest updates, he went for the remote instead, and clicked on the small bedroom TV, knowing Jenn liked to catch the morning news over breakfast, especially when they were sharing it in bed.

It had been a long time since he'd known things like that about a woman, a long time since he'd wanted to know them.

The picture came on first, and he found himself looking at a perky blond news anchor. Behind her, an empty outline of a man's head had a big question mark in place of a face. Below her, the headline read "Key members of the Death Stare task force believe they'll soon have a sketch of the mastermind."

His blood iced. "She didn't."

Then the volume cut in, and the perky blonde reported, "Sources say that a key witness has come forward and is scheduled to meet with a sketch artist this morning. Police Chief Mendoza has called a midmorning press conference, and there's speculation that the sketch will be released at that time. Bear Claw News Ten will have an exclusive—"

"Jenn!" He hadn't meant to bellow her name, but the volume just sort of came out, as did the glare he speared her with when she hurried into the room with a mug in each hand—tea for her, coffee for him—and her eyes wide.

"What…" She caught sight of the news report, which he'd muted rather than hearing the rest. He could damn well guess what was going on, and her quick face-fall confirmed it. "Nick," she began, but then broke off guiltily. After a moment, though, her chin came up and she offered one of the mugs. "I think you're going to want your coffee for this."

His heart thudded sickly in his chest, powered by a complicated mix of anger, betrayal and an inner "oh, hell no." He took the coffee and drank deep, feeling it scald on the way down. It gave his voice an excuse to be rough when he said, "Tell me you didn't pull the trigger on this without talking to me."

She avoided his eyes, cradling her tea mug in both hands as if for warmth, though she was wearing fleece pants and a long-sleeved shirt that clung to her curves. "I was going to tell you about it over breakfast."

"A bribe?"

"Just breakfast." She took a deep breath and looked at him, eyes determinedly calm. "I'm sorry you found out this way, Nick. Maybe I should have woken you up and talked to you about it first…but the thing is, I knew you would try to convince me not to do it."

"Damn right," he growled. "Just like I'd try to talk any jumper off the ledge."

Her look became a glare. "This isn't suicide."

"It's sure as hell not safe."

"Since when do you play it safe?"

Nick muttered a vicious curse at the parallel. "This is about what happened yesterday, isn't it? Payback, Jenn? I scared you so now you're going to scare me, make me prove how much I care about you?" He rose and crossed the room, stark naked, to stand very close to her. He touched her cheek, caught a lock of her hair between his fingers. "You don't need to scare me for that. I care, Jenn. More than I want to admit."

Her eyes clouded, but with more anger than sentiment. "I'm not trying to manipulate you into saying anything, Nick, or feeling more than you want to. This isn't about us. It's about the case."

"Bull." He leaned in, getting in her space to growl, "You wouldn't be doing this if that bomb hadn't gone off."

"You're right, but not the way you mean." She eased back, took a deep breath and said, "It wasn't you getting hurt, or not entirely. It was seeing Trumble's wife and remembering what it felt like to be in her shoes. And it was knowing that the same thing is going to happen, over and over again, if the Investor leaves Bear Claw and sets up somewhere else. Cops. Civilians. They're going to die if we don't take him down, here and now."

And the damn thing was, she was right about that. But she was wrong that she had to be the one to take him down. "You're not trained for this, Jenn."

"No, but I'm the one who saw him."

"Not that you can remember."

"He doesn't know that."

Frustration surged through him. He wanted to grab her and shake her until she regained her senses, wanted to bundle her up and lock her in the safe house until this was all over. He settled with clamping a hand on the back of her neck. "You're not doing it."

Her eyes fired up at him. "You don't get to decide that. What's more, it's already done." But instead of getting really mad, which he'd halfway hoped for—anger was easier to counter than logic—she dialed it back. "I need to do this, Nick. Not just for the case or the city I want to call my home, but for *me*."

"No, you damn well don't."

"I've had to accept that I might not have knowingly let Terry do what he did, but I didn't stop him. And because of what happened, dozens of cases wound up overturned, criminals were released and undoubtedly dozens more crimes happened that shouldn't have."

He tightened his grip on her nape. "You didn't do any of that."

"But I didn't stop it." She lifted a hand to bracket his wrist and hold on, with her fingers over his pulse. "I don't expect you to understand it—I'm not sure I understand it myself, really—but I need to do this. What's more, Tucker agreed with me that it's time. We're running out of options here, and we need to take the Investor down before it's too late."

"Not with you," he grated, but he could feel his grip slipping, not on her, but on the debate. Leaning in, he brushed his lips across hers and felt the ache in his chest swell to a painful pressure. "Please, Jenn. Don't do this. Call it off. For me."

She arched up into the kiss, and the heat they made together was a vivid reminder of last night, when their pleasure had been further sharpened by relief, and the knowledge that he could have been the one spending the night in Critical Care. But when she eased away, her eyes were very serious on his. "You don't get to ask me that. Not if we're just a casual thing."

He froze. "What are you saying?"

"I'm not saying anything."

The pressure turned sharp and vivid in his chest, making the breath rasp in his lungs. "Jenny, please. Talk to me." He didn't know why he was pushing when everything inside him said to pull back, retreat, walk away.

He couldn't walk away from her, though. He'd already tried.

She lifted dry eyes to his, squaring her shoulders as if bracing to take a punch—in this case an emotional one. But her voice was steady. "Okay, you want the ultimatum? Here it is—I'll call Tucker, tell him it's off and agree to lock myself away in whatever safe house you decide…if you promise me that after this case is over, you'll quit the DEA, move here to Bear Claw and give this thing between us a chance."

"You…" His breath hissed out as the blood chilled in his veins. It wasn't a surprise, really, or at least it shouldn't have been. He had seen her face in the waiting room, had felt the difference in her last night. But where he had thought the aching intensity had come from relief, now he realized that on some level, maybe even without realizing it herself, she had been saying goodbye. Quietly, he said, "Please don't do this."

Her shoulders slumped. "You're right that seeing Trumble's wife yesterday reminded me too much what it was like, how bad it could be." Eyes filling, she whispered, "I can't do that, Nick. I won't."

I'm not asking you to. He didn't say it, though, because damn it, he wanted to ask her to do exactly that. Maybe even part of him had been planning on it. "We're good together," he said urgently. "I want to try and make this work." There. He'd admitted it. The raw reality of it dug into his gut, making him want to drag her into his arms and carry her away from the danger. "We can fly to Miami today. Or, better yet, New York. I'll introduce you to my family, show you the theater. We can stay as long as you want." He'd be leaving Tucker behind to solve the case, maybe with a stand-in pretending to be Jenn.

It was just another case, after all, he told himself when guilt tugged at him. But she was far from being just another woman.

She shook her head. "I'm sorry, Nick. I can't do this anymore."

A cold pit opened in his stomach, one that said she was slipping away from him. "You're breaking up with me."

"I'm turning you loose to live the life you've chosen."

"Because I don't want you to use yourself as bait, or because you've remembered what it means to be involved with a frontline cop?"

"Neither. Both." She swiped at her cheek, where a tear had broken free.

The sight cut into him. "Jenny, please. Let's talk

about this. We can work something out." He'd never offered that to anyone else, hadn't thought he would want it for himself.

"I don't think so, Nick." She glanced back over her shoulder to the door. "I need to go."

"Running away?" he asked, hating that it had come to this. Hating that he couldn't have what he wanted

"No. I'm burning breakfast."

It wasn't until she turned and hurried away that he noticed the smell and heard the angry sizzle from the kitchen, the one that warned he wasn't getting any of her special pancakes or bacon today. And apparently never again.

This was it, he knew. This was the end they'd been heading toward for days now, weeks, the impasse that they couldn't breach. He couldn't give up the life he'd built for himself, but he couldn't ask her to share it... not when there was so little to share.

"Perfect," he muttered as he gathered up his clothes and started yanking on his jeans. "This is just freaking perfect." But as he got to his holster and strapped it on with grim intent, he knew that he wasn't going to turn his back on her, no matter what. He was going to watch over her, protect her, and when the Investor came for her, he was going to make damn sure that the bastard went down without hurting a hair on Jenn's head. And after that...

After that, nothing, he knew. He would leave, and both of their lives would get back to normal...except for the gaping hole where his heart used to be.

Chapter Thirteen

Over the next hour, Jenn couldn't decide which was worse, unexpectedly ending things with Nick, or doing it then not being able to get away from him. He was still in the apartment with her, filling her senses and making her want to be weak when she couldn't afford any sign of weakness. Not to him, not to anyone.

She had to be strong right now. Stronger than she'd ever been before.

So far, so good. She'd made it through their discussion without breaking down, though it had been a close call, and then ditched their ruined breakfast, trying not to think how optimistic she'd been while making it or how he'd loved her last night. She'd been fooling herself about him changing. Telling herself fairy tales to make the day ahead seem less scary, while deep down inside she had known they were going to argue, and that it would probably mean the end of their no-strings fling.

After yesterday, she had realized she needed strings. And that couldn't happen with him in Florida, working undercover.

Not that she had thought he would quit for her, not really. Not even to keep her from putting herself out there as a target.

Now, the day ahead wasn't just scary—it loomed empty and hollow without his affection in it. But she could deal with that, just like she had to edge around his big, brooding presence in her suddenly claustrophobic apartment while they got ready. Which included him packing his things without discussion, wordlessly acknowledging that someone else would be coming home with her tonight for guard duty.

The sight of his bags by the door sent a sharp stab through her chest. The emptiness in the bathroom made her hiss out a breath. Seeing the bed, which he'd straightened up some, as if erasing the signs that they'd been together, had her biting back tears. Determination kept her going through the motions, but it wasn't easy.

She knew that wouldn't be the last of it, either. The grief—and the disbelief—had just begun. Been there, done that, had the pity party. And even though she thought it might be a little easier this time because she'd been the one to call it quits, and for legitimate reasons—basic incompatibility trumped great sex, unfortunately—she knew damn well it was going to hurt for far longer than she wanted it to.

Better that than settling for a few more days or weeks of what he was willing to give her, though, knowing she was hanging on to something that wasn't ever going to be what she wanted it to be and, worse, that had the potential to land her back in that waiting room at any moment, waiting to see whether the news would be good or bad.

No, it was better this way.

And if she kept telling herself that, eventually it might ring true.

"You ready to get out of here?" Nick asked from near

the front door. He had his phone in his hand, having just checked in with Tucker and the surveillance teams, and gotten the all clear. His borrowed parka hung open to reveal his holstered pistol and badge, as if to remind her of the danger, and the reason he was really there.

She swallowed past the hard lump of emotion clogging her throat, and croaked, "Ready."

That was a lie—she wasn't ready for them to be over, wasn't ready to open herself up to the Investor's attack. But it didn't matter whether she was ready or not, did it? It was time for her to stop pretending to be brave and actually *be* brave.

The drive to the P.D. passed in silence, with no sign of any tail or danger, making her suddenly question the plan. "What if he's already left the city?" she asked as Nick threaded the SUV through the west side of the city, headed for police headquarters.

"Then you should call this off," he said coolly.

"Is that your professional opinion?"

He hesitated, then cursed under his breath. "No. Professionally, I think you should stick to the plan. If he's still in the area and fixated on you, he'll make his move. If he's already on the run, by the time he hears about the sketch, the press conference will have already been called off, and he'll know you really don't remember anything." He slid her a look. "You don't remember, do you?"

"That hasn't changed." Sure, she had fuzzy impressions, maybe a flash or two here and there, but she couldn't tell at this point if they were real memories or made up to fill the gaps.

He nodded. "Then professionally I think you're doing the right thing. Personally, I want to drive you straight up to that hideaway in the mountains and lock you in there until this is all over." He paused. "It'll kill me if you get hurt, Jenn. Flat-out kill me."

"Nick…" She trailed off, looking out the window and blinking too hard.

Sighing heavily, he shook his head. "Sorry."

"Me, too." She was sorry for all of it—sorry that they had tried again when nothing had really changed, sorry it had worked so well on the surface when the foundation was so flawed, sorry yesterday's reality check had scared her off when she'd thought she was okay with things and very sorry he had found out about her decision from the morning news. Most of all, though, she was sorry that they hadn't made it to their planned goodbye, a kiss at the airport and a wave as he left.

Then again, that probably would've hurt just as badly as this. Because he still would've been walking away from what they'd found together.

Maybe a few months from now she would look back and be grateful for the time they'd had together, which had woken up parts of her that had been numb since Terry's death. Right now, though, there wasn't much in the way of gratitude. It just hurt like hell.

"We're here," he said unnecessarily as he pulled into the parking lot of the P.D. with one of the surveillance teams right behind them.

"Thanks for the ride." She didn't quite choke on the polite words, but she was out of the vehicle almost before he had it parked, beelining for the back door of the P.D., wanting to be inside its familiar, safe walls before anything else went wrong today.

And that was a hell of a thought, considering that

they were only a couple of hours away from a press conference where she'd be making herself a big, fat target.

"Jenn. Wait up." Nick caught her arm just inside the door and urged her down a nearby hallway. "Damn it. We need to talk about this."

She dug in her heels and tugged away. "We *have* talked, Nick, maybe too much. I think it's time to admit that we can't talk our way out of the situation we're in." She paused, softening a little at the dark unhappiness in his eyes. "It's not a crime to want different things out of life."

He cursed under his breath. "I don't—"

"Good. You're both here." Tucker came through from the main lobby with a phone up to his ear and a harried look on his face. "Task force meeting in fifteen, planning for the press conference. Twenty minutes after that, we're transporting Jenn off-site to meet with Alyssa and put the fake sketch together. Normally we'd do that sort of thing here, but we want to give the bastard a chance to…" He trailed off, no doubt getting a look at their faces or catching the tense vibe in the air. Probably both. "Um, sorry. Bad timing, I take it?"

Flushing, Jenn shook her head. "No, it's fine. We're done here." In more ways than one. "Task force meeting in fifteen, you said?" At Tucker's wary nod, she let out a breath. "Okay. I'm going to go down to the lab for a few minutes, then. Drop off my coat, take a breath, that sort of thing."

She didn't wait for Tucker's okay, just headed for the stairs. Part of her was waiting for Nick to call her back. Her feet faltered on the stairs when he didn't, but then she picked herself up and kept going, telling herself it was for the best. This was her job, her career. And today she was going to have the opportunity to impress the hell out of her bosses, and probably secure her position here in Bear Claw.

If she couldn't have everything she wanted, she could at least have this.

The lab was empty, which was a relief in a way. She loved Gigi and the others, but she didn't want to talk right now—not about the plan, and not about Nick. She just wanted a minute alone.

After dropping off her coat and purse in the break room, she sat at her desk and stared blankly at the darkened screen. Today wasn't about the evidence, really. It was about baiting a trap…and once again finding a way to coexist with an ex-lover she was far from over.

For the first time since Nick had come back into her life for real, she was looking forward to the end of the case, not just because it would mean her job review and—hopefully—a new and exciting era for Bear Claw City and its police department…but mostly because it would mean Nick's time there would be over, and he would leave.

She had learned to move on once before; she could do it again.

"Damn it," she muttered, knowing there was no way she was going to get anything accomplished down in the lab today. And nobody could blame her, really. She should be upstairs going over plans and backup plans with the members of the task force.

There was a good chance the Investor would be brought to justice in the next few hours.

Maybe. Possibly. She hoped.

"Jenn?" a man's voice called from the main stairs.

"Sorry to bother you, but Tucker wants you upstairs. They're about ready to start the meeting."

She couldn't place the voice, but saw the uniform pants and heavy boots of an officer. She didn't know all the cops by sight yet, though that was rapidly changing, thanks to the surveillance teams.

"I'll be right up," she replied, feeling suddenly very tired, not just in her body, but in her soul. She hated to admit it, but she really, really didn't want to go upstairs.

Trying not to remember those first few task force meetings after she and Nick had broken up before, and how it had felt as if everyone was looking at her even when they weren't, she hauled herself up from her desk chair, grabbed her cell for taking notes and headed for the stairs.

The officer was waiting for her, making her think that either Tucker had said to make sure she hustled, or else the Bear Claw cops were itchy to get the charade started. Maybe both.

And how weird was it that she was the one about to go undercover? She'd never thought she'd have the guts. She did, though, not only to offer herself as bait, but also to stand up for herself when it came to Nick and what she wanted from him.

When that made her feel a little more in control, she took a deep breath and headed up the stairs. "Thanks for the heads-up," she said to her escort.

"No problem." He fell into step beside her, urging her down the narrow corridor that led past the interrogation rooms and circled back to the conference room, rather than straight across the main lobby. "This way. It's quieter."

A shiver touched the back of her neck, though she

couldn't have said why. Maybe it was because the officer was a little older than the others who'd been keeping an eye on her, with a distinguished air and a bit of gray at his temples. Or maybe it was knowing that she was on the verge of leaving the safety of the P.D., hoping to draw out the killer.

"You ready to do the sketch?" her escort asked as they drew abreast of Interrogation One.

"Absolutely," she answered, sticking to the fiction she and Tucker had agreed would be best to maintain for all but a select few task force members, to limit the possibility of a leak. "In an hour or so, we'll have the Investor's picture all over the place. After that, it should only be a matter of time."

"It's strange you should say that." He caught her arm in a viselike grip. "Considering that the man you're supposedly going to be sketching is right next to you, and you haven't even flinched."

The prickles turned to panic.

He clapped a hand over her mouth and shoved her through a nearby door.

And in that instant, she remembered everything.

She saw a man—this man—coming through the apartment door, into her crime scene, and remembered realizing too late that he wasn't one of the cops. She had lurched to her feet, tried to fend him off, but he'd overpowered her, battering her to the ground with terrifying ease. She remembered lying there, half-conscious and watching through slitted lids as he grabbed the evidence cases and started scouring the apartment for whatever evidence he'd been afraid of having left behind.

He was just coming back toward her, his eyes flat and deadly, when there was a noise in the hallway, one that sent him bolting out the fire escape in an instant, just as Nick burst in and she slipped fully unconscious, not realizing how close she'd come to death and how fortunate she was to be alive.

She'd gotten very lucky that time, she knew now for certain, and her heart drummed sickly at the knowledge that he had her again.

And this time Nick wouldn't be coming to her rescue.

Terror whipped through her at the *thud-click* of the door locking, and she broke from her paralysis, lashing out a kick while she screamed. Or tried to—the noise was muffled behind his palm and his hard grip held her close to his body, turning her blows ineffective.

Worse, as he spun them away from the door, she saw the motionless body of a man wearing uniform pants and an undershirt, no doubt the guard he had overpowered and posed as. There was a dark smear of blood on the floor beneath the young officer, and she didn't think he was breathing. More, the surveillance camera was disabled, the one-way glass covered with a taped-up tarp, warning that this was no spur-of-the-moment attack. He had a plan.

Then her eyes went beyond all that to a duffel in the corner, unzipped to show the unmistakable outline of a digital display and the wires and matte surface of fully armed C-4.

Oh, God. She couldn't think, couldn't react, couldn't deal.

There was a bomb. In the Bear Claw P.D.

She made a muffled noise of horror, and the Investor followed her gaze, his eyes lighting with satisfaction. "Rather neat, don't you think? I'll take care of you and any evidence that could come back to bite me, all at once. And if I gut the Bear Claw police in the process, all the better."

Bile pressed at the back of her throat and the room started to spin, as she was hit with her usual crime scene panic times a thousand. She went limp and weak, making it far too easy for her captor to gag her with a strip torn from the officer's shirt, tie her hands and feet with two other strips of the tough polyester. Then he looped the last strip around one of the bolted-down table legs, tying it tightly enough that her hands and feet tingled.

Trapped. She was trapped. Helpless.

"Not so tough without your boyfriend, are you?" he gloated, making her think of Nick, and how he would've been with her if they hadn't fought.

She was alone, and the only one who knew the enemy was only minutes away from leveling the P.D.

Terror slashed. She didn't want to die, didn't want her friends to die, didn't want the lab destroyed, didn't want any of this.

Focus, she told herself. *Deal with it.* There were dozens of cops just a short distance away. Cops who would be dead in a few minutes if she didn't act fast.

She had to find a way to slow him down and alert the others, warn them. But how?

Think!

JENN WAS LATE FOR THE MEETING, which wasn't like her.

Nick checked his watch for the fifth time in the past few minutes, and glanced over when the door swung open. It was Jack Williams and a couple of other detectives, looking serious and steadfast. Jack shot Nick a look on his way in, sending him a nod, as if to say,

We're on it, buddy. We're not going to let anything happen to her.

Which he appreciated. He just hoped to hell it was all going to work the way they were hoping. He had seen too many ops go bad over the years, though, and the memories had a hard churn knotting deep in his gut.

"Where is she?" he muttered, earning himself a speculative look from Tucker.

The other man hadn't pried, but he was no dummy, either. He had undoubtedly more or less guessed what was going on between Nick and Jenn, but had only said, "I hope you know what you're doing, and you're not just falling back on the familiar stuff because it's, well, familiar." He had grimaced with some not-quite-comfortable memory. "Ask me how I know."

And the thing was, Tucker might've been the original rolling stone back a few years ago, moving cities and departments every few years, always off in search of the next cool scene, the next group of friends…but these days he looked happier than ever, content and settled with Alyssa and their baby girl.

Just because a radical change had worked for him, though, didn't mean it would work the same for everyone. Especially not a guy who had already tried the home-and-hearth thing, and failed spectacularly.

Now, though, Tucker didn't press the point. He just glanced at his own watch, then at the door. "Want me to ask Alyssa to check on her?" Implying that she would probably want to see one of her friends right now, not him.

Which might be the case, but he'd be damned if he went back to keeping his safe, careful distance from her. "No. I'll go."

Tucker shot him a look. "No offense, but I don't think that's the best idea. I can't have two of my key people distracted right now."

Under any other circumstance, with any other key personnel, Nick would've agreed flat-out. Now, though, with Jenn, he shook his head as a new, deep-seated heat kindled in his chest. "You're damn right I'm distracted. But staying away from her isn't going to fix that."

What the hell was he doing? Tucker was right, he had fallen back on old, familiar patterns when things had gotten uncomfortable, without really asking himself whether it was what he wanted. He had just assumed it was, because that was the way he'd lived his life for so long now, alone and adrift. But if that was what he wanted, why was he so miserable now? Why wasn't he counting the hours until he could get out of there?

Because he didn't want to leave, that was why. He wanted to stick around and work things out with Jenn, damn it. Even if it made things really uncomfortable.

Even if it meant changing some of the things he'd considered inviolate for so long. Because somehow those things suddenly seemed a whole lot less important than the woman who had made love to him last night and then burned his bacon that morning, reaching for a new sense of independence, of strength.

Tucker had been watching him, making him wonder what was showing on his face. But the other man said only, "Going after her?"

"You're damn right I'm going after her." Nick rose even as a few more cops trickled in for the meeting.

Hurrying now, he headed for the lab and stopped dead when he saw the empty stairwell. Spinning back, he stuck his head in the reception area and demanded, "Where's the lab guard?"

Kelsey frowned. "Becks? He was there a minute ago." She rose. "Did he bring Jenn into the meeting?"

"No. He didn't." Senses going on sudden high alert, Nick pounded down the stairs. "Jenn? Jenny, darn it, answer me. Are you down here?"

Silence.

His pulse thudded sickly in his veins as he reversed back up the stairs, suddenly very certain that the Investor had made his move and taken the bait, only they hadn't been ready for him. Damn!

Just as he hit the main floor, there was a sudden *screech-thud* from the direction of the interrogation rooms, followed by a man's muffled shout.

Amber erupted from underneath the front desk. Scrabbling on the polished floor, the dog still made it to the door ahead of Nick. She snuffled for a moment at the door, going suddenly tense and edgy. And then, to his horror, she stiffened and alerted, not just of an intruder, but with the characteristic chuff that said she'd scented explosives!

"Amber!" Kelsey had made it to the end of the hall on one crutch, and now her eyes were wide and shocked.

"Stay back," Nick ordered, keeping his voice low and edging away from the door. "And call her off. Then I want you to tell Tucker what just happened, and then get the rest of the building cleared."

"What are you—"

"I'm staying right here." He didn't know what exactly was going on, but he could guess all too horribly who was on the other side of that door.

The Investor…and Jenn. And a bomb.

God. How could this have happened? They were in the damned department! How had the bastard waltzed right in and taken over like this? Taken a *hostage* like this?

Kelsey must have seen from his expression that there was no point in arguing, because she called Amber and the two of them disappeared around the corner.

Which left Nick to ease back down the hallway, straining to hear another noise that might tell him what they were dealing with. He missed a step at the sight of a pale red boot smear on the floor. He didn't know if it was the guard's blood or Jenn's, but the sight sparked new fury inside him.

It was as if everything he'd done up to this point, everything he had learned, suddenly coalesced into this one moment, this one crucially important op.

He had to get to Jenn, had to save her. Had to tell her he'd been wrong and convince her to give him another chance, to give *them* another chance.

He reached the door, laid a hand on the panel and took a breath, trying to settle his fury enough to think, to focus.

He didn't dare make a mistake. This was too important.

"I know you're out there." The voice was muffled by the door, but the tone sent a chill down Nick's spine, warning him that he was dealing with a very dangerous man…and one who had suddenly found himself cornered, making him exponentially more vicious.

Raising his voice, aware that he was about to play the single most important role of his life, he said, "I'm here. The others will be here in a minute. So why don't you and me talk about getting you out of there safely?" He went with Good Cop and added a touch of Conspirator.

He only hoped to God it worked.

Chapter Fourteen

Struggling to breathe around her gag in the wake of the Investor's vicious blow to her face, Jenn whimpered softly and tried to hold down the panic. She had made enough noise to attract attention, but she was afraid of what she might have gotten herself into in the process.

He was furious, muttering to himself and pacing, tapping his temple with the barrel of a .38 pistol he'd produced from the pocket of his uniform pants. She didn't know if he'd taken it from the guard, along with the standard-issue Taser, or if he'd carried it in with him.

At the thought, her mind seemed to kick back into gear, analyzing the evidence at hand and coming up with far more questions than answers. How had he gotten in? How had he gotten the jump on the guard? Did he have someone on the inside of the P.D. helping him?

The idea put a new, sick twist in her gut. She hated the thought of a conspiracy inside the task force, hated that Bear Claw could be tainted like that. More, she hated lying here, helpless, knowing that Nick stood on the other side of the door, only a thin panel away from her captor's weapon, with no information on what he was facing inside the small room.

But what could she do? How could she tell him without endangering them both?

"Hello?" Nick called. "I'm still here, waiting on you. What can we do to get everybody out of this in one piece?"

"Not going to happen," the Investor muttered, still pacing, still tapping away with his gun. "None of you are going to make it out of this. I am, though. I have to."

He kept glancing at the duffel, pacing toward it and away, but always coming back to it with a determination that terrified Jenn.

Don't do it, she wanted to say. *Please don't do it.*

He didn't want to kill himself, that much was clear. But he wanted to do maximum damage on his way out of Bear Claw…and she and Nick were directly in the line of fire.

Suddenly, all the things that had happened over the past two days—seeing Nick hurt, reliving things at the hospital, the two of them picking a fight this morning because it was easier than figuring out how to make it work—all of that seemed so much less important than it had. Now, lying there, helpless and impotent while Nick risked his life to keep the Investor talking, none of the little things mattered nearly so much as the big picture. And in the big picture, she and Nick worked together. They belonged together.

Somehow.

Given that, it seemed all too fitting that she was back in Interrogation Three, where things had started to fall apart in the first place.

Why had she made it all or nothing with her ultimatum that morning? Why hadn't she tried to find some sort of compromise, one that made each of them squirm, but didn't mean he had to abandon the work that was so important to him that he'd given up a big chunk of his life to it?

Was there any wonder he'd turned her down? On the one hand, she was fighting for her career, and on the other, she was asking him to give his up.

How had she not seen that? How had she not recognized it?

I'm sorry, Nick. The words stayed in her head, though, not even making it out as a moan, because at that moment, the Investor barked a vicious curse and strode to the door, which he'd jammed shut with a metal brace.

Pressing his palm to the panel, he said, "I want a helicopter and a pilot in the parking lot in fifteen minutes. Fully fueled, with parachutes." Under his breath, he added, "Damn good thing I'm the only one left. Nobody left to squeal when I take off with you, and light this place up on my way out."

Jenn's pulse kicked. There wasn't an inside man in the task force, after all...but he was planning on taking her with him and setting off the bomb. She couldn't let that happen, wouldn't let it happen. But how could she stop him?

"I can get you a helicopter, have you flown wherever you want," Nick said. "But I'll need a show of good faith. Give me one of the hostages."

"There *is* only one."

Jenn made a low, broken noise around the gag, imagining what Nick must be thinking, what he must be feeling. And also at the confirmation that the guard was dead. She had been hoping against hope he was unconscious, or maybe playing possum.

She was lying next to a dead man. Bile threatened to rise, but she fought it back, refusing to give in to the weakness. Not now, when she needed to be strong.

"I need something," Nick pressed, voice rough with emotion.

Her captor flicked a glance at her, then crossed the room in a few short strides and crouched down beside her.

Jenn didn't let herself flinch back, but that was about all she could manage.

"Go ahead." He jerked down her gag. "Say something. Not," he said quickly, "anything about what's in here." He leaned in close, pinning her with his killer's eyes. "You don't want to make me mad, do you?"

She shook her head mutely, unable to speak at first. But then, knowing Nick would be frantic out there, needing to know she was okay, she moistened her lips and said brokenly, "Nick? Nick, it's me."

"Jenny." The word was an explosion of pent-up breath, of feeling.

She wanted to tell him that she was okay, that she was sorry for pushing him like she had that morning, that she wished she could go back and say something different, something that offered a middle ground. There was no time for that, though. He needed intel, not love words.

"Remember Terry?" she said, hoping against hope that he would understand. "This is nothing like that. None of those lies." *He's working alone. You can trust the others.*

Would he get that? Would it matter to whatever they were planning?

"That's enough!" Her captor shoved her with a booted

foot, then knelt and pulled up roughly on her gag, wrenching it back into place with enough force to make her jaw ache and bring tears to her eyes.

"Okay," Nick said through the door. "Okay, you've got her. I believe you. I want her out of there safely... so how about you tell me what you want?" There was a pause before he said, lower and with a threatening edge, "Trust me, you're better off dealing with me than anybody else you're going to get around here. I'm not a local. All I care about is getting the hostage out of there safely."

The Investor shot a baleful look back at her. "Your boyfriend thinks I'm an idiot. He thinks I don't know who and what he is, why he's in town."

But he was listening, Jenn thought. He was talking. That had to be good, right? Her heart drummed against her ribs and that sick churn stayed put in her stomach, though, because talking was one thing, getting out was another.

Then, just at the very edge of her hearing, she heard a faint buzzing hum coming from over near the guard's body. It sounded like...a drill! The surveillance techs were breaking through, getting eyes into the room.

But just as she realized what was going on, the machine noise changed, growing suddenly louder as the bit hit what sounded like a layer of metal.

The Investor's head whipped up and around.

Jenn coughed wretchedly around the gag, making as much noise as she could. She ran out of oxygen quickly, though, and doubled over, close to panic as her head spun. But she kept coughing, kept masking the sound of the drill.

"What's going on in there?" Nick said sharply. "What are you doing to her? No hostage, no deal. Period."

"She's fine."

"Okay, I'm going to take your word on that. I'm also talking to my people about the chopper. But…listen. What should I call you?"

The Investor hesitated, then turned his attention back to the door and snarled, "You don't need to call me anything." Then, nudging her roughly, he said, "Shut the hell up. I'm not taking off the gag. And if you don't stop, you're going to wish you had."

At that ominous threat, Jenn wheezed to silence, face burning with fear and exertion. But now she could see the tip of a fiber-optic camera nudging through a small hole near the floor.

They were going to break through and try to rescue her. More, they would know that there was a bomb in the room, and that the Investor had a gun.

Relief rushed through her, along with a sudden feeling that she wasn't alone anymore. There would be no flash-bangs or gas. The cops would have to break through and take him by force, and he would know that. He would be ready.

Well, so will I, Jenn thought with a sudden burst of determination that had her tugging sharply at her hands, first one way, then the other. And one of them gave!

Heart racing now, she yanked and then twisted. Her wrist scraped painfully against the table leg, but it worked! Her hand slid free, easing the singing pain in her arm and shoulder and sending her pulse into the stratosphere. She had done it!

The Investor was over by the duffel now, staring down at the bomb and tapping the gun against his temple, making her badly afraid that he was going to arm the device and try to shoot his way out, thinking the explosion would give him the distraction he needed to get away.

It might work, but she wouldn't live through it. And she was determined to live.

Breathing shallowly now, afraid that he would notice what was going on, she started working on her other wrist, hoping against hope that she would be in time. And, more, that she would get a chance to tell Nick that she would find a way to live with the danger, because she knew now that she didn't want to live without him in her life, one way or another.

"THE HELICOPTER IS ON its way," Nick said, pitching his voice to carry through the door. "It'll be here in ten minutes. We need to talk about getting you out to the parking lot."

His hands were sweating where they held one of the monitors that showed the scene inside the interrogation room. *Keep him talking,* he reminded himself. *Keep him with you.*

He didn't like the way the Investor was focusing on the bomb now, or the rapid pacing or the way he kept wagging that gun. He might've been cool, calm and collected in the outside world, when he'd had the former mayor on his payroll and a militia at his beck and call, but now, alone and cornered inside the police department, he was rapidly coming unhinged. And that would make him unpredictable, and exponentially more dangerous than he'd been before.

Now, he whirled to glare at the door. "We're both

coming out. Me and the hostage. I'll let her go when I'm sure I'm out, and that you're not following."

Only he wouldn't let her go, Nick knew. He might not need to kill her to keep her from being a witness—his face was no mystery now, though they still hadn't come up with an ID, despite facial recognition software and the federal databases. The techs were working on it, though. Even given that, though, even if he got onto the helicopter and felt safe, he wasn't going to let Jenn go. Not alive, anyway.

Worse, they couldn't go in after him. Not with the bomb sitting right there, and the techs unable to guarantee that it wouldn't go off if they breached. In fact, they were pretty sure that it would go off if they blasted through the door or walls to get into the room, and suspected the Investor had a dead man's switch on him somewhere, primed to blow the whole building if he hit it.

Which left them waiting and watching, when all he wanted to do was rush in there and save the woman he loved. The one he'd realized too late that he loved, too late that he needed to do whatever it took to make things work between them.

She had his heart; she was his life and his home. How had it taken him so damn long to see it?

Ah, Jenny, he thought, his heart aching in the hollow spot in his chest. She lay motionless near the bolted-down table, bound and gagged, and so damn vulnerable it made him want to tear apart her captor, limb from freaking limb.

He made himself focus, though, made himself play the role. Negotiator was a new one for him, but he'd spent most of his life politicking with the dregs of society. This wasn't much of a leap.

"Okay," he said. "Five minutes to landing. We need to get you out of that room. Tell me how that's going to happen."

Before the Investor answered, though, there was a crackle of radio static in his earpiece, and Tucker said urgently, "Nick, we've got him. He's had some work done, which is what slowed things down, but we freaking got him. His name is Robert Iskander, and he's bad news from way back. Originally out of the Eastern Bloc countries, he's got an Interpol sheet and wanteds in half a dozen countries. The feds didn't even know he was in the States, he was flying that deep."

"Okay," Nick said, though it was anything but. This guy wasn't just local bad news, he was international bad news. And he had Jenn. "Okay, let's do this." It was time to bring Iskander out of the room. "Everybody back off. And I mean way back."

On the monitor, Iskander bent and adjusted something in the duffel, making Nick's blood run cold.

"He's armed it," one of the techs reported tersely. "We've got two minutes on the display."

"Can you disarm it?"

"If you get me in there right now? Maybe."

Pulse thudding in his ears, Nick called through the door, "The chopper's about to land. Are you coming out?"

He tensed as Iskander moved over to Jenn, yanked on her bonds and dragged her to her feet, where she wavered and sagged momentarily before she managed to brace and stagger a couple of steps on her own.

Fury flooded Nick's veins. Pure animal rage. He was shaking with it, seeing bloody red with it.

"We're coming out." Iskander moved to the door and pulled the bar out from under the handle. He kept his gun trained on Jenn the whole time. "I'd better not see anybody out there. This is just between you and me."

Nick waved the others away, tossed the monitor to one of the techs and moved back a few paces himself. "Okay. You're clear."

The lock rattled and the door swung open, and his heart lodged in his throat as Iskander emerged, keeping Jenn in front of him as a human shield. Her eyes were wide and dark, stark in her bloodlessly pale face, which was red-streaked with a forming bruise.

"You bastard," Nick rasped. "If you've hurt her—" He bit off the words, which hadn't come from the Negotiator or the Good Cop, or from anywhere but the man inside him.

Iskander smirked. "Like I said. When I'm sure I'm safe and nobody's following me, I'll let her go." He gestured with the gun, in the direction of the parking lot, where the low *thwap-whack* of an incoming helicopter was just becoming audible. "Shall we? And although it should go without saying, if you try anything—and I mean *anything*—she dies."

Nick could feel the seconds ticking away, and knew he was stalling, using up crucial seconds on the bomb, so it would go off just as he made it to the chopper. "You're in charge," he said through gritted teeth. "You're getting what you want."

The bastard's eyes darkened. "Not hardly. Not—"

"Nick, *now!*" Jenn cried suddenly. And she twisted,

grabbed Iskander's gun hand and sank her teeth into his wrist.

Her captor yelled in surprise and pain, and reeled back in stunned surprise. Nick didn't hesitate. He roared and threw himself on the bastard, driving a fist into the Investor's stunned face and pummeling him away from Jenn.

They hit the wall and caromed off, punching and struggling.

"In his pocket!" Jenn shouted. "He's got a remote!"

As the bomb techs raced into the interrogation room, Nick tore at Iskander's pockets, found the unit and tossed it to her. "Get it to the techs!"

"No!" Iskander reared back and went for Nick's throat, eyes bulging with rage and the dawning knowledge that he was close to being beaten. "No. Impossible!"

The two men flailed and crashed into the opposite wall, and something plastic went skittering away. *Taser,* Nick thought, and was damn grateful the bastard had lost his grip on it. He had a good hold on Nick's throat, though, and a hell of a grip. Nick slammed him into the wall, trying to inflict maximum damage, maximum pain, again and again.

And then, finally, Iskander's grip slackened and his eyes went groggy and glazed.

Nick let go of him, let him fall in an inglorious heap on the polished hallway of the interrogation area, and sucked in a ragged breath as a dozen officers swarmed Iskander, slapping restraints on him and searching him roughly for more weapons.

"The bomb," Nick croaked.

"Neutralized," came the call from inside Interrogation Three. "The remote had a kill switch."

He didn't want to sway on his feet, but couldn't quite stop the floor from moving. "Jenn?"

"Here!" came a soft cry from behind him.

He turned as she came flying toward him, and they met in a rush. He clamped his arms around her, buried his face in her hair. "*Jenny!* God. I thought…"

"I know. I know. I thought it, too." She kissed his face, his throat, his chin, anything she could reach. Tears streamed down her face, but her eyes were clear and bright, those of the warrior who had gotten out of her bonds and helped take down Iskander before he'd set a foot outside the police department.

"You were brilliant," he said roughly, catching her mouth with his for a bruising kiss that didn't do nearly enough to convey what he wanted to say to her. "You *are* brilliant. You're wonderful. Amazing. Everything I could ever want and more."

She pulled away, tears coming in earnest now. "I shouldn't have pushed like that," she said in an emotion-choked voice. "I was asking you to give up everything for me, even though I wouldn't do the same thing for you."

"It doesn't matter. I'll quit. Now. Five minutes ago. Whatever it takes. I love you and I don't want to walk away from you ever again."

"It *does* matter. And I don't want you to quit. You love what you do. You're the best at it. You…" She trailed off, freezing. "You what?"

"I love you, Jenn. I'm sorry it took me so long to figure it out, but I do. And I'm going to do whatever it takes to make this work, even if that means trading in my badge."

"No." She framed his face in her hands. "Don't."

His heart twisted in his chest. "Don't what? Don't love you?"

"Don't quit. Not yet. We'll figure out something that works for both of us, somehow."

The pressure in his chest eased. "And?"

Her face lit like a sunrise. "And I love you." She threw her head back and laughed aloud. "I love you! It feels so good to say that, to know it and not be afraid of it anymore." Easing back into his arms, she kissed him, then whispered, "I'm not afraid anymore."

"I should hope not. You just took down an internationally wanted criminal. What's there to be afraid of?"

She grinned up at him, with all the love in the world shining in her eyes. "Nothing, as long as I have you by my side."

Epilogue

One year later

An early-winter storm had whipped down from the mountains to blanket Bear Claw in a layer of snow, but not even the nose-nipping bite of the wind was enough to cancel the groundbreaking ceremony for the new police headquarters.

As Matt Blackthorn—now thoroughly ensconced as the city's progressive, reinvigorating mayor—climbed up on the temporary stage with Gigi at his side in her role as the First Lady of Bear Claw, a breeze sprang up, making Jenn shiver a little despite all the layers she was wearing.

"Here." Another, heavier layer draped suddenly over her shoulders, folding around her with masculine body heat and the smell of leather and man.

She snuggled into the familiar bomber, instantly warmed, though she looked up and over her shoulder, laughing at Nick with a token protest. "You'll freeze!"

"What do you think I am, some sort of wimpy Southern boy?" Clad only in a base layer and a heavy navy blue fleece, he didn't look at all uncomfortable as he wrapped his arms around her and leaned down to rub his cheek against hers. "I may be a transplant, but I've adapted."

"Yeah," she sighed against him. "You sure have."

A year ago, she never would have believed that he could be happy quitting the DEA and settling here in Bear Claw with her, but that was exactly what he'd done. And not once had he thrown it back at her that he'd been the one to make more of the changes to make their relationship work. If anything, when she brought it up, he brushed it off and said he was just grateful she was willing to put up with him and Ransom, the K9 officer he'd paired up with soon after he'd joined the Bear Claw P.D. full-time.

She wasn't just putting up with man and dog, though. She loved them both, and couldn't imagine her life without them. Didn't want to.

Yes, he was still on the front lines of the action, but that had been her compromise. Besides, things had been relatively quiet since the Investor's arrest. He'd wound up being extradited, which had been just fine with the Death Stare task force. Their enemy looked to be getting several consecutive life sentences at a minimum, and the residents of Bear Claw had gotten some breathing room, as had the police force and its analysts…which now included Jenn, full-time and locked in, which was exactly where she wanted to be.

When she wasn't at home with Nick, that is. They had only been married a few months, but things between them didn't show any signs of slowing down. If anything, she fell more and more in love with him by the day, though it seemed that should have been impossible.

As Matt started his brief speech by thanking the local businesses that had donated to the construction project, along with the administrators of the federal grant that had matched the donated funds, Nick grinned down at her and arched one eyebrow. "What? You're staring."

"I'm crazy about you." She didn't mind saying it now, didn't mind feeling it. Not when she knew it was utterly mutual, that he was just as much in love with her as she was with him. Not when the future stretched out in front of them, gleaming with promise. They were still living in her apartment, still talking about what kind of house they wanted, what kind of family, but they were talking about it, planning for it.

And that was something she hadn't ever thought she would want again, a puzzle piece she hadn't ever thought she would find.

"I'm a damn lucky guy," he said, and turned her in his arms so he could kiss her for real, sneaking his hands beneath the heavy weight of his jacket, so their shared body heat warmed the little pocket of air they made between them. His lips were cool at first, but heated quickly, reminding her of just where they had left things that morning, and where they would pick up later tonight.

She moaned a little into his mouth, but then laughed as a heavy weight bumped their legs, chuffing a little as Ransom jostled his way into the embrace, interrupting the moment. Which was probably just as well, as they were far from being alone.

"I'd like to invite a few friends up here with me to help get this project off the ground," Matt said into the microphone. "You know who you are. Come on up!"

Nick nudged her in the direction of the stage. "That's your cue."

"Here." She handed back his jacket with a kiss. "I'll be right back."

Ransom whuffed after her but stayed put as she made her way up to the stage, meeting Alyssa, Cassie and Maya at the steps, along with several of the local and federal-level cops who had been instrumental in bringing down the Investor, and several other major crime sprees before that, all of which had hinged—either directly or indirectly—on the problems in the mayor's office.

Now, though, those days were gone. Mayor Blackthorn was tough but fair, and he had big plans to make the city safer and more prosperous by the year. Starting with the new police department, and the crime lab they were breaking ground for today.

The new, shiny, fully tricked-out and—most important—*aboveground* crime lab.

The agents, officers and detectives stood back, letting the members of the Bear Claw Crime Lab gather near the mayor, who stood near an oversize ribbon and a faintly muddy section of earth that had been salted for the occasion.

As Jenn joined her friends at what would become the front door of their new lab, she looked down into the crowd to lock eyes with Nick. He beamed at her and gave her a thumbs-up, and there was nothing but love and acceptance in his eyes. He didn't need to play roles anymore; neither of them did. They were who and what they were, and those people worked together, clicked together, and loved each other. Here, in Bear Claw.

"And now," Matt announced, "let's do this!"

Together, the members of the crime lab snipped the

ribbon and, laughing, took muddy scoops of dirt, ceremonially dumping them off to the side.

And, as they split off later, each of the analysts teamed up with the men they had met and married there, in Bear Claw. Nick and Jenn were among the last to leave, lingering with Matt and Gigi for a long time, enjoying the wide-open construction area and the promise of the years to come. Eventually they moved off, though, with Ransom tagging at their heels, his tail sweeping in wide, happy wags.

"Home?" Nick said as he held the door of their SUV for her.

"Definitely," she said. "Let's get out of here before somebody forgets we're both off shift, and gets it into their heads to put us to work."

He laughed and shut the door, then came around to the driver's side, saying as he climbed in, "They wouldn't dare."

Dispatch would, but she had a feeling they were going to get lucky today, and have a few hours together uninterrupted, maybe longer. "Still, let's hightail it home," she said, savoring the word and leaning into him as he pulled out of the parking lot.

Bear Claw was her home now. More, Nick was her home, and a future she hadn't even known she wanted until she finally learned how to fight for what she needed…and the future they both deserved.

* * * * *

He was looking for adventure…and he found her.

Kate Hoffmann

brings you another scorching tale

With just a bus ticket and $100 in his pocket, Dermot Quinn
sets out to experience life as his Irish immigrant grandfather
had—penniless, unemployed and living in the moment.
So when he takes a job as a farmhand, Dermot expects he'll
work for a while, then be on his way. The last thing he expects
is to find passion with country girl Rachel Howe, and his
wanderlust turning into a lust of another kind.

THE MIGHTY QUINNS:
DERMOT

Available August 2012 wherever books are sold!